# JINGLE BELLS, RIFLE SHELLS

## A SMILEY AND MCBLYTHE MYSTERY

# Other books by Bruce Hammack

## The Smiley and McBlythe Mystery Series

*Exercise Is Murder*

*The Long Fall*

*The Ice House Murder*

# JINGLE BELLS, RIFLE SHELLS

A Smiley and McBlythe Mystery

# BRUCE HAMMACK

Published by Jubilee Publishing, LLC
ISBN-978-0-9884408-8-3

Cover design: Streetlight Graphics
Editors:
    Teresa Lynn, Tranquility Press
    Kit Duncan

# CHAPTER 1

How long has your husband been missing?"

Steve Smiley waited for the answer as he sat at a conference table on the third floor of the McBlythe Professional Building in The Woodlands, Texas.

Heather McBlythe, Steve's partner in their private investigation firm, settled in a high-backed leather chair. She lifted a Mont Blanc pen from a yellow legal pad and wrote the date and time in small, neat strokes. If things went as hoped, she and Steve would be working on a missing person case that afternoon. Not the type of case Steve specialized in, but at least it would occupy his mind with something besides Christmas. He loathed Christmas.

Margaret Lee, their potential client, looked trim and in good health. At seventy-plus years, she had a full head of hair the color of polished silver. Wrinkles around her eyes spoke of years mixed with joy and sorrow. Only the blue-veined, liver-spotted hands led Heather to believe the woman had reached her seventh decade of life.

Mrs. Lee reminded Heather of her own grandmother.

Steve repeated his question. "Mrs. Lee, your husband, has he been missing long?"

Margaret's forehead wrinkled in thought. "Oh, dear. Let me see. How long has Tom been missing? Two days? Three? Yes, three days."

With a trembling voice, she pleaded, "Please help me find Tom."

"We'll do our best, Mrs. Lee," said Heather. "Are you sure you wouldn't like coffee or a cup of tea? You must be very cold after that walk across the windy parking lot."

The woman scanned the office a few seconds longer than necessary. Ignoring the question, she said, "This is a lovely office. You two must be very successful."

"We do investigations part-time," said Steve. "Heather spends most of her time pursuing other endeavors. How did you hear about us? We don't advertise."

Heather made a note that Margaret Lee looked off once again.

Her gaze returned to Heather. "I love the way you decorated for the holidays. I also noticed your name is on the building. Do you own it?"

Heather nodded. She needed to get the woman on track. "Mrs. Lee, Mr. Smiley asked how you heard of us."

"I'm sorry. I thought I told you." She flicked a hand. "No matter. I read about you in the newspaper. You solved a case for the police. I think they called it The Ice House Murder. I found you online and made the appointment. Thank you for seeing me on a Saturday." She took a close look at Steve. "How long have you been blind, Mr. Smiley?"

Heather stopped writing. The question of Steve's loss of vision didn't seem to catch him off guard, but he had long mastered the art of not revealing what went on behind his sunglasses. Few people ever asked or mentioned it.

"Not quite three years," said Steve. "Has your husband gone missing before?"

"No." She paused again for a few clicks longer than normal. Her eyebrows knitted together. "I seem to recall something that happened to him a long time ago, shortly after we married." Her gaze shifted to stare at one of Heather's framed diplomas. "Or was it before we married?" She smiled like a loving grandmother. "I'm afraid my memory isn't what it used to be."

"Is your husband on any medications?" asked Steve.

"Oh, no, he's in perfect health. Pilots have to be in top condition. He has perfect eyes, a great physique, and is very handsome."

"Does your husband still fly?" asked Steve.

She looked off to the wall again. "Of course, Tom flies. He's a pilot." Her voice trailed off. A blank stare remained fixed on Heather's law school diploma. Margaret reached into a purse of abundant size and pulled out a framed photo. A film of tears clouded her eyes. "I brought a picture of Tom. I knew you'd need it." A shaking right hand delivered it to Heather as if it were a possession beyond price.

Heather looked at the photo and drew in a deep breath. Flanked by the American flag and the flag of the United States Air Force, a keen-eyed young officer sat for the photo in his dress blues. For Steve's sake, Heather said, "I'm holding a photo of an exceptionally handsome Air Force Captain, circa 1969." She placed the photo into Margaret's outstretched hand.

"Ahh," said Steve. His voice lowered. "Is this the most recent photo you have of your husband?"

"I have some snapshots in my room. They're photos of Tom and the other pilots outside their tents. Oh yes, there's one photo I'm particularly fond of. Tom's looking out to a rice paddy. It's a lovely shot of his profile."

Heather's cell phone sounded an alert. She'd forgotten to turn it off. After reading the message, her first attempt to speak caught in her throat. On the second try, she said, "It's a Silver Alert for a missing elderly woman. Her name is Margaret Rosenbaum."

Margaret looked up from the photo. "Oh, my. I hope they find her." A puzzled look came over her countenance. "Rosenbaum? Why is that name familiar?"

Her gaze fixed again on the fifty-year-old photo and remained there.

Heather excused herself, rose from her chair, strode out of the office and eased the door shut. After completing the call to the Montgomery County Sheriff's Office, she placed the receptionist's phone in its cradle.

Heather's thoughts turned to Steve. When he realized Mrs. Rosenbaum's husband had died a half-century earlier, his hands curled into a fist, and the muscles in his jaw flexed. His mood had shifted from expectant to sullen and despondent. Almost three years had passed since he lost Maggie. The pain from her murder haunted him every Christmas as if it were one of Dickens' ghosts. Talking to a woman living in a world that existed fifty years ago wasn't what he needed. The holiday funk had settled in him like a case of the flu. Heather had to do something before he drifted into full-blown depression.

# CHAPTER 2

I don't know where we are, but it isn't anywhere near our townhomes," said Steve.

After the morning's fiasco, Steve had given voice to what he planned to do the rest of the day. He couldn't wait to get home, put on sweats and binge on listening to anything that didn't involve Christmas.

Heather slowed her car to a crawl. "We're in the north parking lot of The Woodlands Mall," she said.

Steve expelled a huff of disgust. "You know I hate malls. I can't think of a worse place to spend the day than in a crowded mall."

Heather didn't reply as noise assaulted her car. A car alarm sounded a short distance away. A battle of blaring horns began when two drivers jockeyed for the same parking spot. Steve shifted in his seat for the third time in as many minutes. If she didn't get him walking soon, he'd bail out and call UBER.

"What are we waiting on?" His voice held the edge of a serrated knife. "Get out of here."

Heather inched the car forward and braked hard. A man and woman, their arms loaded with purchases, crossed in front of the car. The man scowled at Heather and mouthed a complaint about pedestrians having the right of way.

"What was that guy thinking?" Heather exclaimed. "He walked right out in front of me."

"Only crazy people go to the mall the Saturday after Thanksgiving."

"Here we go," Heather said with relief. "A yellow Porsche 718 Boxster is backing out. Cool car. I've been thinking of getting something sporty for Christmas. What do you think?"

The question didn't earn a response.

Heather's Lexus SUV shot forward, swung in a tight arc to the right and came to an abrupt stop.

"We made it," said Heather in a voice that sounded too chipper, even to her. "Let's go."

Steve didn't unhook his seat belt. "I'm staying here."

"No, you're not. It's time you rubbed elbows with the masses and absorbed some peace on earth and goodwill toward men."

He faced forward, his molars grinding. "Do you have any idea how much I hate Christmas music?"

"You used to like it, didn't you?"

"You're not listening. I don't like it now."

"I bet Maggie loved it, didn't she?"

11

He turned to face her. His voice skipped like a car driving over a washboard gravel road. "Yeah, she loved Christmas, and I acted like I did too."

Heather turned to face him. "You pretended?"

Steve's words rushed out. "All right, counselor. I confess. I did enjoy Christmas, but that was before. I didn't protect Maggie. She's gone, and I'm blind. I'd prefer to sleep from mid-November until New Year's Eve. Sounds relating to Christmas remind me of her." His voice intensified in volume. "Do you know the best thing about being blind at Christmas?" He continued before she had a chance to give a lame answer. "I can't see the decorations, I can't see the stupid sweaters people wear, and I can't see couples holding hands."

Steve moaned a sigh of regret for his outburst. The few times she'd witnessed him slip into self-pity, he'd regretted it.

She looked away from his tortured countenance. The missing person case could have given him something to concentrate on other than Maggie. That turned into a cruel joke. Heather heard the "Holly-Jolly" strains of Christmas music. The car passing behind them broadcast Yuletide spirit loud enough for the entire parking lot to hear.

Steve took off his sunglasses and rubbed his eyes. "I'm sorry. You deserve more than to have me ruin your Christmas. I hear Maggie's voice singing with the carols and hymns."

Heather swallowed hard. She'd heard him talk about Maggie, but not like this.

He replaced his sunglasses and drew in a full breath. "Maggie was my wife for over twenty-five years. She had a love of Christmas that was second to none. On Black Friday Maggie rose before first light. She put on tennis shoes and sweats and elbowed her way through the hordes of shoppers. The Saturday after Thanksgiving was sacred in our home. She reserved it for decorating. I should be wrestling lights around a prickly tree and listening to her sing along with Bing Crosby or Alvin and the Chipmunks."

He shook himself out of the memory. "Take me home."

What should she do? Allow him to go deeper into memories or treat him with a firm hand? She faced him and selected between two bad options.

"Come on!" Heather said with a firmness that surprised even her. "You've managed to get stains on most of your shirts. I'll not tolerate a business partner whose clothes look like the apron of a short-order cook. We need to do something about your ongoing love affair with all things fried. In the meantime, you're getting five new shirts today. No arguments."

Steve huffed out a breath of surrender and wrapped his neck with a scarf. "I'll go, but only if you take me to the food court first. You dragged me to the office before I had a chance to finish my breakfast."

"Deal."

13

# CHAPTER 3

Cold wind stabbed Heather's ears. Steve's hand rested on her shoulder, and they walked toward the sounds of people and music. The voices of noisy shoppers grew louder the farther they walked. The tip of his cane found a curb, and he lifted his foot high enough to clear it.

The booming voice of a man and a teenage girl broke through the ending of *Rudolph the Red-Nosed Reindeer*. The man stood tall and stout with hands tented on his hips. He wore camo from cap to boots. He shouted, "Don't argue and don't you dare talk to me in that tone. You're going to wear it, and that's final."

"It's freezing. How can you expect me to wear that thing in the middle of winter?" The girl's stance mimicked the man, with hands on hips. Their eyes locked in mutual defiance.

The "No, I won't—Yes, you will" argument grew louder the closer Heather and Steve moved toward the squabble.

What sounded like a hand slapping a side of beef preceded the explosion of a gunshot by a heartbeat. It blasted through the argument and the chorus of *Frosty the Snowman*. The man crumbled to the sidewalk.

Time stopped. Heather ducked from under Steve's hand, reached up and pulled him to a squatting position. Silence fell on the crowd, but only for a few seconds. Pandemonium erupted. A few people screamed and ran to the parking lot. Most sprinted toward the entrance of the mall.

Steve's fingers dug into Heather's shoulder. "Take cover!" His shout echoed off the building. He shouted the command again, louder this time. The stampede intensified.

Heather noticed Steve's cane searching for answers. It touched the foot of the downed man. The leg twitched, but only once.

"Heather, we have to get out of here," said Steve.

"There's no way we can get into the mall. Too many people are jamming the doors. Hang on to me. We're going toward the street."

"You're taking us directly toward the shooter," said Steve.

Heather's voice came out a half-octave higher than usual as she grabbed the girl's coat. "We have to leave him. It's too dangerous here."

Heather turned to Steve. "There's a van coming. I'll stop it."

15

She looked at the girl and judged her to be seventeen or eighteen. Heather took Steve's hand and placed it on the shoulder of the girl. Heather's gaze bore into the girl's eyes. "I'm going to stop that van. When it gets here, get him behind it. Don't leave him and keep low."

Steve had his cell phone in hand. He gave it a simple command. "Call 911."

Heather bolted into the street and stood with palms raised in the path of a tall van. Tires screeched, and the front bumper brushed her slacks. "Get out!" She shouted the command to the driver of the van and his passenger. "Take cover behind the van. Someone's shooting."

The occupants complied, and Heather crouched behind the van's front wheel. The girl and Steve settled beside her. Steve had his phone on speaker.

"Montgomery County 911. What's the nature of your emergency?"

"One shot fired at the north entrance of The Woodlands Mall. One person hit and down. I'm a retired Houston homicide detective. Relay to responders that they are to treat this as an active-shooter situation." His words came unhurried and calm, using the cop voice he'd developed two and a half decades ago. He answered as many of the dispatcher's questions as he could.

Heather took his phone and expounded on the information he'd given the 911 operator. "Hold EMS until the area is secured. I'll stay on the line."

A lull in the conversation gave Heather a chance to replay what they'd experienced. She and Steve had walked due south from her car. It had to be south because a twenty-mile-per-hour north wind nipped at their backs. A Salvation Army bell-ringer had been to their left, near the main entrance to the mall. The man lying on the sidewalk and the girl crouching beside Steve had been arguing. A slap? No, it wasn't a slap. It had to be a bullet striking flesh. A loud boom followed.

"Steve, any idea of the type of rifle?" she asked.

"Not an ordinary gunshot. Too loud. Big caliber."

She tried to focus on her memory of the gunshot's thunderous sound.

"Heather."

"Yeah."

"Tell them the shot came from somewhere beyond the north mall parking lot. Also, tell them to roll something with armor. The rifle is a larger caliber than anything our guys will be carrying."

Heather relayed Steve's message and added, "You'd better get some units here quick. A couple of civilians are coming out of the mall with pistols drawn. They're checking the downed man. They're shaking their heads. Have officers enter the mall from the south doors only."

Sirens screamed their advance. Steve turned his head to the teen. His words eased out in a matter-of-fact tone. "You must be the young lady having a difference of opinion. What's your name?"

17

The girl looked at the man lying prostrate on the sidewalk and said nothing.

# CHAPTER 4

An eerie quiet fell over the scene. Heather hadn't noticed the round lens of a camera pointing at her. How long had the guy from the van been filming? He'd heard the 911 conversation. Great, Steve hated publicity.

She noticed the graphics on the side of the van and looked at the woman with press credentials hanging from a lanyard. "Mind turning that thing off?" asked Heather.

The woman ignored the request and launched into questions. "What's your name and tell us how you two know so much about police procedures."

Heather turned away, allowing her auburn hair to drape the side of her face.

"Habib," the reporter huffed. "Keep getting shots of the front of the store and the cop cars."

The camera swung around, but the questions didn't stop. "Why isn't EMS here? What are the cops waiting for? The guy might still be alive."

The teen's next words came with unexpected surety. "He's dead."

Heather looked at the girl full-on for the first time. She wasn't an average teen. Her looks and bearing went far beyond that. Thick silvery-blonde hair fell in a braided rope to her waist. She had a presence about her that far exceeded her years.

"It's too dangerous," said Steve, answering the reporter's question.

"Your name, sir?"

"Smiley. Steve Smiley."

"Why did you say it's too dangerous? That's what they get paid for, isn't it?"

"You haven't been a reporter long, have you?" asked Heather.

The reporter couldn't have been older than twenty-six, four years younger than Heather. She didn't respond with words, but her scowl told Heather the lack of experience had hit a sore spot. Raven hair, so black it shimmered, lifted and fell in the swirling wind on the lee side of the van. Her eyes resembled round lumps of coal. She wasn't tall but had curves, noticeable even though she wore a jacket. Her face, flawless as a handkerchief of tan silk, framed naturally full red lips that formed a perfect cupid's bow. They were the kind of lips Heather didn't want to risk Botox injections to achieve. The reporter's lips looked natural.

Steve broke the silence. "First responders take enough risks. They don't get paid to walk into an ambush. In a case like this, they'll wait for an APC."

As if on cue, a military surplus armored personnel carrier lumbered toward them. The six-wheeled vehicle spun, backed over the curb and came to a halt about ten feet from the fallen man, shielding him from further attacks. The sound of rear doors opening overpowered the Christmas carols that continued to play, incongruent with the grizzly scene. Helmeted men in full tactical gear exited the rear of the APC. The reporter narrated as the cameraman recorded images.

Heather, still in a crouch, moved past the reporters as one of the men in full tactical gear sprinted to her. "Are you Smiley?" he asked.

"I'm Heather McBlythe. I used to be a cop, too."

"Dispatch told us Smiley might have eyes on the shooter. Any idea where the shot came from?"

Steve answered for her. "I'm Smiley. Check the roof of the building at your ten o'clock. It should be about two-fifty to three-hundred yards away."

The man took a look at Steve's sunglasses and cane. He gave Heather a questioning look.

She nodded. "Do as he says."

The marksman scanned through the scope of his sniper's rifle. "Nothing," he said. The business end of the rifle swept left and right with the same results. "Are you sure it was the roof of the pet store?"

Steve pointed with his cane. "I'm sure it came from ten o'clock."

"Roger. Any idea what he used?"

21

"Not an AR, an AK or anything shooting a NATO round. Not a .308 or anything else in a thirty caliber. Low humidity and the north wind carried the sound to me. It made more of a boom than a crack. It's a big caliber, but it didn't sound like a Barrett fifty cal."

The sniper relayed the information. He stayed next to Heather with the rifle's bipod resting on the hood of the reporter's van.

The armored vehicle ground forward and slipped off the curb. Reporter and cameraman bolted from their position and ran in the APC's wake. It passed beyond the mall's parking lot and across a blocked-off street.

"Idiots," whispered the sniper as he watched the reporter and cameraman expose themselves.

"If you have binoculars or a spotter's scope, I can help you scan," offered Heather.

Without lifting his head from the rifle, the SWAT sniper slipped binoculars to her.

The lumbering APC came to a stop in front of the pet store. Once again, it discharged its load. The men bolted inside. Minutes passed.

In the background, Heather heard Steve speaking in calm, reassuring tones to the girl. To this point, the girl had remained virtually mute and displayed no tears.

The sniper standing beside Heather gave a running commentary, punctuated by long breaks of silence. "The entry team's clearing the store. Three went out a rear door. They had to get a ladder tall enough to reach a metal ladder attached to the exterior of the building.

They're on the roof. No sign of the assailant." His voice increased in volume. "They found the rifle and a spent casing. The roof and store are clear."

Patrol cars representing law enforcement agencies in the county and some from adjoining Harris County streamed into the cordoned-off area. A full contingent of state troopers added to the number. The first of many unmarked black SUVs joined the assembly. Two men and a woman with FBI printed on their ballistics vests came to a quick stop and took cover behind their vehicle. The long, laborious task of securing the crime scene and investigating the shooting awaited multiple agencies.

The police sniper backed away from the van and pocketed the binoculars Heather handed him. "Good call on the rifle." He said it loud enough for Steve and the girl to hear.

Heather raised her eyebrows in surprise when the girl asked, "What caliber was it?"

When the sniper hesitated, Heather said, "Might as well tell her. She'll find out soon enough."

"A .416 Remington Magnum."

"That's an elephant gun," said Steve.

The girl added, "I hate it. Kicks like crazy." She looked at Heather. "Are you a cop?"

"I used to be. I'm an attorney and a private investigator."

The girl's loose strands of long hair danced in the wind. "Is the blind guy your dad?"

Steve let out a moan. "You sure know how to hurt a guy's feelings. I don't look that old, do I?"

The girl looked at her feet. "Sorry." Her chin lifted. "If she's not your daughter, who is she?"

"My business partner. We conduct investigations together."

Heather looked into the girl's glacier-blue eyes. "Are you going to tell us your name?"

"Bella Brumley. You've seen me on TV if you watch the outdoor hunting channel."

"Who's the man that was shot?" asked Steve.

Heather hadn't noticed, but the sniper had moved out. He'd made it thirty yards into the parking lot, heading for the pet store.

Bella ignored the question. "Can I hire you?"

Heather jerked her gaze toward the girl. Slender, tall, gorgeous. Scandinavian descent, she guessed. "Why would you need us?"

Bella pointed to the man covered with a silver blanket. "That's my dad. Well, not my real dad. I'm adopted. The police are going to think I had something to do with this."

# CHAPTER 5

The arrival of another black SUV put any further conversation on hold. The six-foot-six-inch frame of Montgomery County Sheriff's Captain Charles Loving slid out of the driver's seat. Heather greeted him with a two-armed hug and a question. "Are you in charge?"

"I am for now. The sheriff's stuck in Houston traffic."

He shifted his gaze to the teen and returned it to Heather. "She looks familiar. Is she a witness?"

"She's more than a witness. Her name's Bella Brumley. The victim is her adoptive father. The three of us were nearby when he went down."

"Brumley? Blake Brumley?"

Bella stood to her full height of six-feet tall. "I'm right here. Why don't you ask me?"

Charles Loving stumbled over an apology. His radio crackled out his call sign, and he turned away.

Heather moved to Bella and spoke low. "Were you serious? Do you want me to act as your attorney?"

She nodded.

Steve jumped in. "Did you have anything to do with this?"

"No, but never mind. I'll tell you later."

Heather's brows drew together. She wasn't about to wait for an explanation. Leaning into Bella, she spoke in a low voice, "Did you make plans to kill him?"

"No, but I didn't like him. The cops will find that out as soon as they check my Facebook account. Are you a good lawyer?"

"She's the best," said Steve.

Bella looked at Steve and returned her gaze to Heather. "I like him." She issued a one-word job offer that sounded more like a challenge. "Well?"

"Let's talk for a few minutes before we decide," said Heather. "You might not like me, and I may not want to represent you. For the time being, don't talk about any problems you had with your father. The police only need to know what happened today. Don't give them a reason to detain you."

"Where's your mother?" asked Steve.

She shrugged. "Beats me. Somewhere in the world killing something." She looked at the ground. "She's not my mother. And he wasn't my father. I was their business acquisition. He bought out my adopted mom's share of me in their divorce settlement."

Heather took Bella by the hand. "How old are you?"

"Eighteen."

Heather tilted her head and looked hard into Bella's eyes. "Try again. How old?"

Her head dipped. "Almost seventeen."

"You look older."

"They portray me as being eighteen in the commercials I shoot. That way, they can show me buying ammo and picking out rifles and shotguns. Blake even got me a fake driver's license showing me as eighteen."

One more time, Heather's mind raced. The girl referred to her adoptive father by his first name. He wasn't Dad, only an impersonal man named Blake. The adopted mother didn't rate a name. Bella might well be eighteen in the eyes of the viewing public, but she had the legal status of a juvenile. Giving the police enough information to satisfy them would be tricky.

While Heather rolled things over in her mind, Steve asked. "Is there a next of kin we can call?"

"Nobody." The answer came with speed and conviction.

Heather reached a decision. The girl needed help. "Do you have that license on you?"

A cell phone with a card carrier attached came forth from Bella's jacket.

"Let me have the license. You don't need to get caught with something illegal on you."

Bella grinned. "I like you, too. Thanks for being my lawyer." She looked at the boots sticking out from under the silver blanket. "Since you two are private

27

investigators, do you think you could find my real parents?"

The enormity of what Bella asked combined with a twenty mile-an-hour north wind gave Heather the shivers. "Let's get out of this cold." They leaned into the gale as a mobile command center pulled to a stop shy of the mall entrance. It looked like an oversized RV emblazoned with the logo of the Sheriff's Department.

The trio retreated to the relative warmth of Heather's SUV. "Sit in the front," said Steve to Bella.

Heather blew into her hands and rubbed them until they achieved a semblance of warmth. It would take a few minutes for the heater to blow something besides chilled air. The heaters in the seats would also take a couple of minutes to warm the leather. "Aren't you cold, Bella?"

"Huh?" Bella didn't maintain eye contact. "Sorry, I've never seen a person die before."

Heather reached out her hand and took Bella's left hand. "I asked if you were cold."

"This isn't cold. Try riding two hours on a snow machine, sit another hour in the snow, and shoot and field-dress a caribou north of the Arctic Circle. That's cold."

Steve chuckled. "Heather, can't you remember how cold Boston gets?"

"I guess my blood thinned from the sweating I did this past summer."

Heather turned in her seat to face Bella. She hadn't noticed it, but a crimson birthmark, the size of a postage stamp and shaped like a mushroom, occupied a spot under the girl's left ear. She made a mental note of it.

"The police will want to interview you after they get the command center operational," said Steve.

"No problem. I'm great at giving interviews."

"This will be a different type of interview. We don't want you to be too good. Tell us why you and Blake Brumley were here today."

The sixteen-year-old seemed to age in front of Heather's eyes. Her diction became crisp and clear while her posture telegraphed a level of self-assuredness not present in most adults, let alone a teenager. She spoke as if she was reciting a television commercial.

"Daddy and I are here today to make sure you will be the first to have access to his new book, *The Art of the Kill.* And get this, I'll be modeling selections from our new outdoor clothing line." Like a game show hostess, her hand swept the front of the coat she wore. "Check out my super-warm triple-insulated, lightweight jacket with a matching pink vest. Don't miss the special camo swimsuits I'll be revealing (big wink) at four o'clock."

She took a breath and returned as a sixteen-year-old. "That's why we were fighting. That bikini barely covered me. Besides freezing, I didn't want a bunch of snuff-dippers drooling and making those sounds guys make. I told Blake he could wear the stupid thing."

29

"That must have been the conversation you were having when we approached you," said Heather. "If the police ask you about the argument, tell them you were having a difference of opinion about advertising. If they ask you to explain, I'll take over."

Steve spoke from the rear seat. "They're bound to ask if you know of anyone who'd want to harm Blake."

"Hmph. That could be a long list. Start with his ex-wife, Jolene Brumley. Wait, she uses her maiden name, Jolene Cox."

"How long have they been divorced?"

Bella repositioned her braid over her right shoulder and began to examine the gathered ends of her hair. "I don't know. They pretended they were still married on the show until I turned fourteen. Blake replaced her with me."

Steve's leather seat crunched as he leaned forward. "You mentioned before that Jolene might be somewhere killing something. What did you mean?"

"She started her own big game hunting business. Jolene finds people with more money than they know what to do with and takes them on hunts. The more rugged the hunt, the more she likes it. She's twice the hunter Blake was, but she stinks in front of a camera."

"Does she own a .416 Remington Magnum?"

"Yeah." She paused and cast her gaze up and to the side the way people do when they're pondering. "At least she used to." Her eyelids narrowed. "That's the rifle that went missing."

"When was that?" asked Steve.

"Ages ago. I was twelve, almost thirteen. We returned from filming somewhere in Africa. A rifle case didn't make it to Houston. Jolene caused a huge scene at the airport."

"And Blake?" asked Heather.

"He told Jolene she had a problem. We grabbed our gear and left her to deal with baggage claim. That's the way he was, only concerned with Big Blake. I think the airline found the rifle and returned it. I don't know if Blake gave it to Jolene or not. I don't remember seeing it after that trip, but Blake has tons of rifles." Her head dropped. "I guess I should say Blake *had* tons of rifles."

Heather looked out the windshield and spoke to herself as much as to the other two. "If I have to, I'll give the police Jolene's name. It will save them a few steps." She turned and looked at Bella. "I won't do it if you don't want me to. I'm trying to show you have nothing to hide. If they have something to follow up on, our chances of getting out of here soon will increase." She swiveled in her seat. "What do you think, Steve?"

"I'd like to get us into Bella's home before the police get there with a search warrant."

Bella answered Heather's unasked question. "Jolene means nothing special to me. Tell the cops what you think is best." Her tone wasn't malevolent, only mature.

Steve asked, "Who does mean something to you?"

31

"I liked my nanny, or au pair, or teacher, or whatever you want to call her. Her name is Gwen Fontaine. Blake fired her a few months ago. She'd been with me since I was four. I miss her a lot." Bella's eyes brightened. "Of course, there's Mike."

"Mike? Is he a boyfriend?" asked Steve.

The child in her came out as she giggled. "You could say he's my boyfriend, but not like Dart was. Mike is my cocker spaniel."

"Who is Dart?"

"His name is D'Artagnan, but everyone calls him Dart. He used to be my sort-of boyfriend." She paused. "I'm using the term *boyfriend* loosely. We never really dated, but he flirted with me quite a bit."

Something like tape ripping from skin seasoned Bella's last sentence. Heather asked, "He used to be your boyfriend? He's not any longer?"

"No. Blake shot him."

A sheriff's deputy tapped on Heather's window. Clarification would have to wait. A cold blast of air and an instruction met her as the window descended.

"Captain Loving needs you three to come to the command trailer."

# CHAPTER 6

The reporter managed to position herself with the front of the mall, police tape, and a portion of the command trailer captured in the background. Captain Loving stood with a microphone near his chin. Still forty yards away, Heather saw the microphone slip into the reporter's jacket pocket. She reached with both hands, pulled the Captain's face to hers and gave him a smoldering kiss.

Heather swerved into Steve. Their feet tangled.

"Hey!" said Steve. "I'm walking on these feet. Find your own."

"Wow," said Bella. "I didn't know cops kissed like that."

Heather corrected her course, but not her emotions. They remained a twisted mess. Her stomach did a few somersaults, bringing to mind a flight with a navy pilot she'd once dated. He thought it would be a good idea to do a few snap rolls to show off. The relationship ended that day with him having to clean a very messy cockpit. She set her jaw and increased speed.

Captain Loving's eyes widened when he saw the trio approach. He quickly disengaged himself from the reporter. She spun in time to see the group of witnesses to the shooting as they approached. Microphone in hand, she tried to block their path. "Captain Loving says you saw what happened today. Tell our viewers what was going through your mind."

"No comment," said Heather through clenched teeth.

Steve followed with, "Sorry, I didn't see a thing."

"What about you, Bella? Do you have anything to say to your fans?"

Heather cut Bella off before she had a chance to utter a sound. "Miss Brumley has no comment."

"She's of age," challenged the reporter. "Why can't she speak for herself?"

Heather kept walking, remembering a saying she'd learned the hard way as a rookie cop. Never engage in a battle of words with someone who could cut and splice what you said. She looped her arm through Bella's and whispered, "Keep walking."

Once they traveled several yards past the reporter, Heather asked, "Can you cry on demand?"

"Sure, my acting coach taught me how to do that."

Heather leaned into her and gave instructions. "You're an emotional wreck because of Blake's death. Call him Dad or Daddy. If I pull my ear, turn on the water-works. I don't plan on us staying here any longer than we have to."

34

Steve had the hearing of a fox. Being blind served to heighten his other senses. He chuckled when Heather spoke of her plan to make their stay in the command trailer as brief as possible.

"Three steps up," said Heather to Steve. His cane told him how high to step. They filed into the trailer and took seats around a table.

Captain Loving placed a hand on Bella's shoulder. "Let me begin by saying how sorry we are for your loss."

The actress in her came out as she hung her head and mumbled a meek thank you.

Heather didn't allow Captain Loving to sit before she said, "You should know that I'll be representing Ms. Brumley." Her stomach did another somersault as she noticed a substantial amount of lipstick on his mouth.

Captain Loving's head tilted as he eased into a chair. "I was hoping to keep this interview informal as a courtesy."

"I think not," replied Heather. Her gaze fixed on a spot between Captain Loving's eyes.

Out of the corner of her eye, Heather saw a deputy look at her. The woman must have known they'd been dating for several months. Heather straightened her posture. She needed to get out of Charles' presence before she made a fool of herself.

Captain Loving asked Heather to tell what she'd seen and heard. Using as few words as possible, she relayed the events. Steve followed, but could only say what he'd heard.

"And what about you, Ms. Brumley? Why were you and your father outside the store?"

Heather pulled on her ear. Bella began to sniffle. Her head drooped, and her hands clenched together so hard her fingers turned white. "Blood, there was so much blood."

"I know this is hard, but we need to catch the killer," said Captain Loving.

"Hard?" said Heather with accusation stabbing the word. "Her father was killed right in front of her." She kept talking at a quick clip. "Bella is a tough young woman, but can't you see she's in shock? Steve and I have already spoken to her. She and her father went outside to discuss issues related to an advertising campaign. They were working out details on swimsuit modeling she was to do this afternoon."

"I heard there was an argument."

"Nothing but two creative people exchanging their opinions."

Bella's tears flowed unabated. She began to breathe in quick bursts.

"Is that all?" asked Heather.

The captain lowered his voice to a whisper as if he hoped Bella didn't hear him. "Did she happen to say who might have wanted to harm her father?"

"Check out her adoptive mother, Jolene Cox."

Bella wailed and bent over, her braid draping onto the table.

Heather rose. "A .416 Remington Magnum belonging to Jolene Cox went missing several years ago. Bella doesn't know if she now has it." She pulled Bella to her feet. Steve followed suit and rose from his chair.

"I'll need a complete statement from Ms. Brumley tomorrow."

"Come by my office tomorrow afternoon," said Heather

A turn of his head indicating confusion followed her statement. "That's not how things are done."

Heather issued the coldest stare she could. "That's the way things will be done if you want our cooperation. You decide, Captain." She paused. "By the way, Bella will be staying with me for the foreseeable future. If you need to talk to her, contact me first." Heather took a step toward the door. "We're through." Charles Loving could take her last statement to mean whatever he wanted to.

# CHAPTER 7

The reporter waited at the bottom of the steps with the cameraman capturing images of those descending. "Alexandria Ramos reporting from the police command center at The Woodlands Mall. Here is Bella Brumley, co-star of *Big Blake's Big Game*. Are the police any closer to capturing your father's killer?"

Heather whispered, "Don't slow down. Keep wailing and walking."

Once inside her car with her two passengers, Heather rested her forearms on the steering wheel and leaned forward. Her stomach gurgled, and the first twinge of a headache came to her left temple.

"How did I do?" asked Bella.

"You did great," said Steve. "You're an amazing actress."

"Was Heather serious about me staying with her?"

"We need to take you to your home so you can get some clothes. Heather and I will have a lot to do, and we'll need to have you near."

"A lot to do? Like what?"

Heather felt as if her emotions had been through the spin cycle of a washing machine. She sat with eyes closed and only half-listened as Steve continued.

"The most immediate thing is to keep you from being detained for arguing with your father. A suspicious cop might say you lured him outside so someone you chose could shoot him. Besides that, you have an interview with Captain Loving tomorrow afternoon. We'll need to coach you on what to expect. Heather has to rearrange her schedule so she can devote her time to you. By the way, where do you live?"

"About thirty minutes from here, near Cut and Shoot."

"That figures," said Heather as she leaned her head against the rest. "Leave it to Texas to name a town Cut and Shoot, and for a big game hunter to live there."

"Blake thought it would be good marketing," said Bella. "Why can't I stay at my house? I can drive to wherever you need me to be."

"No way," said Steve. "Heather's keeping your license. If you were to get pulled over with that, the cop would run it and find out you're only sixteen. You'd be placed in foster care or living with your adoptive mother. You don't want that, do you?"

"Yuck."

Heather looked in the rearview mirror. "Help me, Steve. My mind is mush. What else do we need to do?"

"We need to go to Cut and Shoot as soon as possible. It shouldn't take long for the cops to get a search warrant, but we might have an hour or so to look around before they get there. Think about what legal papers you might need to make copies of."

Bella turned to face Heather. "They're bound to be in one of Blake's gun safes. I have the combinations to them."

"We also need to start thinking about arranging a funeral," said Steve.

"By *we*, do you mean me?" asked Heather.

"I'll do it." Steve didn't allow her to respond before he continued. "The best way for us to get the heat away from Bella is to find whoever shot Blake. Until that happens, we'll play dumb and let people continue to think she's eighteen."

"What else?" asked Heather.

"Lighten up on Captain Loving. I don't know why you talked to him the way you did, but stop it."

"But—"

"But, nothing. He owes us for solving the ice house case for him. I want you to call him and apologize. Tell him we'll be glad to take Bella to his office tomorrow."

Bella couldn't keep quiet. "That cute little reporter laid an R-rated kiss on him. I bet that's why Heather's wrapped so tight."

"Ah-hah," said Steve. "*Cherchez la femme.* Still, Heather, we can't be making an enemy out of an asset. Swallow your pride and call him."

Before Heather could respond, Bella said, "Mike's coming with me. I'll need to get his food and doggy toys."

Steve's chuckle rose. "It will be interesting to see how he and Max get along."

"Max?"

"Heather's Maine Coon cat."

Ignoring his comment, Bella said, "And don't forget the most important thing. You need to find my mom and dad."

Heather groaned.

Steve's voice lowered and became somber. "That may be a long shot, Bella. Even if we find either of them, there's no guarantee they'll want you in their life."

"Mom will. I know she will."

Bella didn't lack confidence, but Heather had her doubts. "What makes you so sure?"

"I'm rich." The words rolled off her tongue. A window into the mind of Bella Brumley flew open. She saw herself as a commodity, an asset on the left side of a ledger. Her birth mother would want her because she could bring what Blake Brumley wanted from her. The money she could produce.

Bella brought Heather from her ponderings when she said, "There's one more thing we need to get for Heather, but I'm not sure where we can find it."

"What's that?" asked Steve.

41

"She needs a great big bandage on her broken heart. That tall, handsome cop and the cute reporter did a number on her today."

Heather spun in her seat. "Young lady, you'd do well to consider your words before you speak. My heart is off-limits, and while we're getting things straight, you're to call me Miss Heather or Ms. McBride. Understood?"

"Jeeze, you don't have to bite my head off."

Heather turned to Steve. "How about it? Do we take the case?"

"Solving a murder and tracking a missing parent or two is better than listening to Christmas music. What do you think?"

"I'm ready to make a certain captain I know look like a fool. How do I get to Cut and Shoot?"

"Go north on I-45. You'll turn right at Conroe," said Bella.

Steve added his comment. "Listen for screams and gunshots. That's how you know you've arrived at Cut and Shoot."

Heather mumbled, "Who in their right mind would name a town Cut and Shoot?"

# CHAPTER 8

Towering pine trees, verdant and thick, lined the roads in and around the town with the bizarre name. National forest land lay to the north and east of the hamlet. Turning off a blacktop road onto a similar driveway, Heather stopped at a keypad on a curved metal pole. For Steve's benefit, she said, "It's a privacy gate with an arched entry. Both are ornate iron. The arch has a sign reading Big Blake's Big Game."

Thoughts of Charles Loving continued to course through Heather's mind as did the memory of the kiss she'd witnessed. Things had been going so good with Charles. When did this other woman come into his life?

"Don't get your hopes up about the place," said Bella. "Blake wanted a fancy entrance with metal cutouts of big game animals. There are only twenty acres. The house is like the front entrance, built to look impressive on TV. Our shooting range is first class, but that's because we do a lot of filming here. I think I've spent half my life on that range."

"How old were you when you started shooting?" asked Steve.

"Three. Blake had a BB gun custom made for me. I don't remember it, but Blake put some framed pictures of me shooting it in the great room."

"And you've been shooting ever since?"

"When I was five, he had me shooting a .22. Each year I'd learn to shoot higher caliber guns. I'm a walking encyclopedia on rifles, shotguns, and ammunition."

Steve tested her knowledge. "Tell me about the .416 Remington Magnum."

Bella pivoted in her seat. "Whoever killed Blake knows how to shoot. The most common round for that gun is a 400-grain bullet. That's two to three times more lead than is used to kill white-tail deer. If the shot came from the roof of the pet store, it traveled at least two-hundred-fifty yards. A 400-grain projectile drops almost thirteen inches at that distance. Of course, you can adjust the elevation on the scope. Since the wind blew directly from the north, the shooter didn't have to account for drift."

"The rifle didn't have a scope," said Steve.

"How do you know that?" asked Heather.

"While you were concentrating on the interview in the mobile command center, I was eavesdropping on a conversation between a Texas Ranger and an FBI agent."

Steve rolled right into the next question for Bella. "Did Blake teach you how to shoot?"

"He didn't have the patience. I learned a lot from the pros the firearms manufacturers would send out with new models. They'd teach Gwen and me, and she made sure I practiced. Uncle Owen helped when he could."

"Who's Uncle Owen?" asked Steve.

"He's not my uncle, that's what I call him. He was our pilot until Blake fired him."

Heather rounded a curve, and the house came into view. "Wow. That's a big house. Impressive."

Bella shrugged. "It looks huge, but the wings on each side are like fake fronts on a movie set. Blake wanted his home to appear bigger than it is."

She explained the construction. "The front of the home is made out of D-logs. They're called D-logs because of their shape. Logs are cut in half and milled so they all look the same. The fronts of the logs are rounded, but the backs are straight. It resembles a log cabin, but it's nothing like the pioneers made."

"From the outside, it reminds me of super-sized Lincoln Logs," said Heather.

The front door boasted the carved relief of a bugling elk with an eagle circling overhead. Bella punched in a code to unlock the front door. An excited ball of fur met the trio as soon as the door swung open. Bella went to her knees and gave the toffee-colored cocker spaniel a rubdown from floppy ears to rump.

Heather scanned the room while Bella and her furry boyfriend finished showering each other with affection. The vaulted ceiling, covered with tongue-and-groove

45

knotty-pine, rose to at least forty feet. Floor-to-ceiling windows flanked each side of a massive rock fireplace. Lifeless eyes from the head mounts of a big game menagerie stared at the cavernous great room from various directions. Heather wondered how spooky it would be to walk into the room on a stormy night when the electricity had been knocked out.

Bella noticed Heather staring at the mounts. "We do a lot of filming here. The rest of the house isn't near this impressive, especially the bedrooms. Mine is only big enough for a twin bed."

Steve tapped the tip of his cane on the hardwood floor. "It sounds like a hundred people could fit in this room and still leave room to dance."

Bella said, "There's room for the film crew to put together multiple sets. We film most of the closings of the shows with the fireplace as a backdrop. That leaves plenty of room to shoot four or five commercials. The room is nothing but a stage." She scanned the room. "It was designed for work and hosting parties."

Heather pointed to glass-fronted gun cases, each empty. "Where do you keep the firearms?"

"They stay locked in gun safes in the basement until it's time to do a shoot or go to the shooting range. It depends on who our sponsor is as to what we bring out. You don't want a Winchester in the background if you're trying to sell Smith and Wesson."

"This is creepy," said Heather as she peered into a glass-enclosed case of snakes. It reminded her of an oversized arcade machine with the metal claw that came down and latched onto cheap toys or stuffed animals. This display didn't have a claw, but it had a collection of reptiles. Heather shivered at the sight of lifelike venomous creatures. "They look alive."

Bella joined her as she stared at the all-too-lifelike creatures. "Those are the world's deadliest snakes. Scary, huh? Blake had them posed to look like they're going to strike the mouse. See the little door in the glass? It's big enough for you to put your hand inside the display. Blake played a game with guests. He'd bet them they wouldn't reach in and grab the mouse in the center."

"Cute game," said Heather.

"That's not the best of it. There's a remote control that activates the snakes. The snakes move a little, but the King Cobra strikes. The fangs look real, but they're made of rubber."

"I bet that gives the guests something to remember," said Steve.

Bella shook her head. "Sales and marketing. Blake said, 'I don't care if they love me or hate me, as long as they remember me.'"

"This is quite a business," said Steve.

Bella turned and began walking. "All business, all the time. Follow me. We'll start looking for the legal stuff you said you needed."

# CHAPTER 9

Heather and Bella made for the basement with Mike's four paws and one wagging tail in front of them. He made it to the bottom of the stairway, scurried to a corner and settled on the hide of a Yak, the only floor covering in an otherwise undecorated room. Bella pulled out her cell phone and punched the NOTES icon. One by one, she dialed in combinations and opened each safe, starting with the one she knew to contain legal papers. Heather viewed television contracts, merchandising agreements, and records of overseas travel. She also scanned a bevy of communique to and from foreign countries. In a separate safe Heather found years of tax filings. She tasked Bella with making copies of some of the tax returns and certain other documents. Almost everything appeared related to forging a good living from the business of hunting and all that accompanied it.

Heather glanced at Bella as she copied a recent agreement Blake had made with the distributor of the line of swimwear. Heather frequently dealt with large sums of money, but the amount in the contract caused her to read the document twice to make sure it wasn't a typo. Could this be the contract that had sparked the day's argument? Funny, the dispute on the sidewalk seemed a long time ago, even though only a handful of hours had passed since Blake Brumley's demise.

"Bella, I can't find any records about you," said Heather. "No school records, no history of shots of any kind, or any medical records. Could they be somewhere else?"

"Gwen home-schooled me and kept all kinds of records. I don't know why we haven't come across those." The bright light from the copy machine seeped out the edge as another copy spit out the side of the machine. "I have no idea what Blake did with my shot records. I know I had enough to kill a Rhino. You wouldn't believe what a hassle it is to travel as much as we did."

Bella tilted her head and asked, "Are you and Mr. Smiley a couple or something?"

Heather shifted her gaze from a stack of papers. "That's getting close to being none of your business."

"Sorry. No need to snap at me." She refocused on making copies. "Blake said I didn't come with a filter on my mouth."

Heather rubbed a knot in her right shoulder. There was no reason to be crabby with Bella. Even though she'd only known the girl for a few short hours, the teen had already displayed directness in her speech. What popped into her mind came out in the form of words, sometimes indelicate words. Heather pondered the question. Was it so out of bounds? After all, Bella had been raised in an adult world, and she would be sharing Heather's townhome.

Heather took in a breath and said, "I'm sorry I snapped at you. Since you'll be staying with me, I'll give you the short version of our relationship. Mr. Smiley and I are not romantically involved. He has his life, and I have mine. We work together when there's a case to solve. Otherwise, I work full time as an attorney and with my father in our family businesses."

"What businesses?"

"There are too many to keep track of. I come from a long line of financial wizards. We turn piles of money into bigger piles. My parents live in Boston."

"Piles of money? How big?"

"That's not important. Keep copying."

Heather's thoughts raced back in time to how her partnership with Steve began. She'd been recruited by Steve seven months earlier at Houston's police academy where he occasionally taught. Her wealthy father had tried to direct her into the world of finance and taking the family fortune to new heights. She'd rebelled and chosen the life of a police officer. It took years for Daddy to act, but when he did, things changed fast. Phone calls went to the right people, and Heather found herself drummed out of the Boston Police Department. She relocated to Houston, intending to start over. Dear old Dad proved to be more persistent than expected. The same story, second verse, came to pass. Phone calls to influential people caused her to be dismissed from the police academy. Homeless and broke, she needed three months before her financial ship docked. When she turned thirty, a trust fund would be at her disposal. There would be more zeros on the numbers transferred to her bank account than she would ever need. Steve had come to her rescue with a spare bedroom, board, and a small stipend until her bank account exploded with funds. He also needed her help in solving a murder.

She'd eventually reached a compromise with her father on how to divide her time. She'd look for investments to keep Daddy happy and, she'd also work with Steve whenever they found a case worthy of their attention.

Heather returned to the present and looked to Bella. "Let me finish answering your question about Steve and me. He has a townhome next door to mine. Our floor plans are mirror images. We put in a pet door between our two dining rooms so my cat can visit Steve whenever he wants. For the most part, Steve lives his life, and I live mine. Is that enough information for you?"

"I still don't know much about either of you."

"We'll talk later. We need to stay busy looking for something that will tell us about you."

"Google me. You'll get my entire history."

"Not quite. Why are none of your records in any of these safes? Where is your passport? There should be adoption records. Who were you before you were Bella Brumley?"

# CHAPTER 10

Steve sat in a chair fashioned from a whiskey barrel. In front of him loomed the glass-enclosed display of snakes. It gave Heather the shivers to look at them. Steve, of course, had no way of knowing how terrifying and lifelike they looked. "What did you find?" he asked.

"It's what we didn't find," said Heather. "There's nothing about Bella in any of the safes other than her name on contracts."

"Hmmm." Steve ran a thumbnail across his chin. "There has to be a file cabinet, or a locked desk drawer, or another safe. Did you find tax records?"

"Bella made copies of them."

"Did you look for a wall safe?"

"I checked behind pictures. The basement is concrete floors and, there's nothing on the walls. We opened the gun safes and searched them thoroughly. I checked under wooden benches covered with short pile carpet to put weapons on so they don't get scratched."

"What about carpet or area rugs?"

"There's one hairy Yak hide tossed in the corner of the basement. Mike seemed fond of it. He wasn't happy when I moved it. No floor safe. The floors in the rest of the house are hardwood or porcelain tile. I tapped for hollow spots and looked for trap doors. Nothing. We went through every room. Blake's office desk had recent projects he was working on, but nothing on Bella except what she would do to promote products. No passport, no shot records, no school records, and no adoption papers."

Steve raised his chin. "Where's Bella? I didn't hear her come downstairs."

Heather settled herself in the twin of the chair Steve occupied. "She's gathering her clothes and personal items."

"You missed something." Steve's matter-of-fact tone wasn't condemning. "There has to be another place he kept records." His head froze the way a horse does at the sound of something approaching. "Cars are coming. I bet it's the deputies. Perhaps they'll have better luck in finding Blake's stash of documents than we did."

Before Heather could open the door, a fist pounded, and a man hollered, "Police! Search warrant." The door flew open. Led by a thick-bodied officer sporting two chevrons on his sleeves, a quartet of deputies entered the room.

"Who are you? What are you doing here?" Accusation seasoned the syllables of a thick East Texas drawl coming from the leader of the pack.

It had been a long day, and Heather's nerves were stretched to their limit. She held out her hand, palm up. "My name is Heather McBlythe. I'm Bella Brumley's attorney. If you have a search warrant, I'll need to see it." She paused. "What took you so long?"

A flush of red colored the corporal's cheeks. He made no move to turn over the search warrant. "I need an I.D. and proof you're an attorney." He turned to the deputies. "Get going. Start on the second floor and work your way back here. You know what to look for."

Steve rose from his chair. "Don't forget the basement. That's where you'll find most of what you're looking for."

The man stood with legs spread wide, too wide. He threw his head back as if to give the impression he looked down on the world. The man's name tag read Gowdy. He reminded Heather of a detective she knew when she worked for the Boston Police Department. The one who'd been promoted one pay grade past his ability.

She mumbled as she retrieved the requested items from her purse. The corporal perused them longer than necessary and keyed a microphone. After dispatch returned his badge number, he said, "I need a 10-29 on a female, last name McBlythe."

Steve took his position next to Heather. He spoke over the man's radio transmission. "You'll save yourself time and grief if you contact Captain Loving. Wants and warrants will come back clean."

The corporal released the transmitter button and stared at Steve. "Who the heck are you to tell me how to do my job?"

Steve held up his left palm in a sign of surrender as his right hand steadied his cane. "Don't say I didn't warn you." He turned to walk away.

"Hold on, you. I need your driver's license."

Steve shook his head and kept walking, his white cane leading the way.

Heather issued Officer Gowdy an unblinking stare. "A driver's license? For a blind man? Are you serious?"

"Look, lady. Maybe you're a lawyer. Maybe you ain't. Maybe you should be here, maybe you shouldn't. Either way, I have a warrant, and I've been told to search and secure this home. If you don't mind joining your friend, I'll be checking a few things. If you are who you claim to be, I'll let you look at this warrant."

Before he could key his microphone, one of the deputies came downstairs with a firm grip on Bella's arm. "I found this one packing a bunch of stuff."

Heather came within three inches of the corporal's face. "That young woman is Bella Brumley. She lives here. Her father was killed this afternoon. Tell your officer to get his hands off her, or you're going to think every animal in this room came back to life by the time I'm through with you."

The officer's eyes narrowed as Heather reached for her cell phone. "You've been asked to call Captain

Loving. If you won't, I will." She stood with index finger poised to press.

The officer kept his eyes on Heather. Uncertainty flashed across his face. "Let her come down on her own." He took a step away from eyes intended to intimidate and reclaimed his bravado. "Bring me what she was packing."

Bella rubbed her bicep and moved to where Heather stood. Both assumed a posture of crossed arms.

The officer rifled through a travel bag and announced, "Nothing leaves this house."

Heather tented her hands on her hips. She opened her mouth to give the man a substantial piece of her mind, but Steve cut her off. "If you'll tell your men to go downstairs they'll find the gun safes are unlocked. Bella did that as a courtesy. One of them contains legal papers. We assume that's what you came for."

"What about computers? That's on the warrant, too."

Bella said, "Blake's computer is in his office. So is his laptop. My laptop is in my room."

Heather followed Steve's lead and backed away from a full-on verbal assault. She said, "I called Captain Loving on our way here. I told him we'd fully cooperate. Is that too hard for you to understand?" She gave him another hard stare for good measure. "I think I'll call Charles so you can explain why you haven't shown me the search warrant yet. I don't think he'll be too happy."

Steve said, "I saw to it that nothing left this home. I give you my word as a former Homicide Detective."

57

Heather had to cover her mouth to keep a snicker from escaping. Steve's quip passed through one of Gowdy's ears and out the other without touching a single brain cell.

"I guess there's no reason to bother the captain," said Gowdy.

Steve whispered something to Bella. She moved to a cabinet and slipped something into her coat pocket.

Steve took a step toward the officer. "There's something I should tell you, officer."

He corrected Steve. "It's Corporal Gowdy."

"I'll write myself a note so I'll remember that." said Steve.

Heather bit hard on the inside of her cheek. Another reference by Steve to his blindness had sailed through the corporal's brain. Could the man be that slow to catch on?

Steve continued. "Heather and Bella have already searched the entire home for documents. We'll be discussing what they discovered with Captain Loving tomorrow afternoon."

A red tint rose in the officer's face. "You had no right to do that."

"Are you an attorney?" asked Heather. "Bella lives here and has full access to everything this side of the front gate."

"The gate," said Steve. "That's what took you so long. You didn't have the code to get in the gate."

Bella added to the conversation. "The fences around this property are made of used drill stem pipe. How long did you wait until you remembered to call the fire department? They have the code."

The corporal's eyes narrowed as his face flushed red.

Heather shook her head in a sign of unbelief. "Back to the warrant. Ms. Brumley gave me her permission to search. Until I'm shown that warrant, I can continue."

He reached a hand inside a tactical vest.

Heather took the document, gave it a cursory inspection, and returned it. "You'll find the records as we found them. All I have are copies that I will take with me. I give you my word as an officer of the court that I am removing only copies of what you will find downstairs."

Gowdy's eyes shifted left and right as if he were looking for an answer lying on the hardwood floor. The speed and certainty of Heather's words must have overloaded his mind.

Bella broke into his confusion and coached him on what to do next. "I heard a rumor that Blake liked to hide documents in unusual places. We haven't checked the mounts on the wall."

Heather watched as Gowdy's eyes scanned the dozens of stuffed heads.

Bella continued. "I believe you'll find something there." She took a step toward him and locked her blue eyes on his gaze. Her voice couldn't have sounded more sincere and innocent. "I heard there's an easy way to find out which mount has the secret stash. If you reach into the snake display and lift the mouse, the mouth of one animal on the wall will open."

Gowdy moved toward the display. His gaze shifted from one deadly reptile to the next. "I ain't puttin' my hand in there."

Heather brushed past him. "Let me do it if you're too scared." She opened the latch at the base of the display and swung open the door. Her hand inched toward the mouse. "See? Nothing happens. They're fakes." She withdrew her hand.

With bravado running at full throttle, Gowdy brushed her aside. "I'll get it." He turned to the officer who had brought Bella downstairs. "Keep an eye on the mounts. Look for a moving mouth."

Heather looked to the balcony as another deputy had his cell phone trained on Gowdy. She nodded to the man whose grin threatened to touch both ears and motioned him to come for a closer shot of what was to come.

Her gaze shifted to Bella. The teen slid her hands in the pockets of her jacket and stared at the display.

The corporal's hand moved into the snake display at the pace of a drugged turtle. Inch by slow inch, the curled fingers approached the mouse. A bead of sweat appeared on Gowdy's top lip. Fingers flexed to grasp the stuffed rodent. The Hooded King Cobra struck with astounding speed. Heather gasped. Her reaction paled to that of Gowdy's.

"Eeee! Eeee! It got me! It got me!"

"Quick, sit him in a chair," said Steve.

"Help! Help!" he bellowed.

"Stay calm," said Bella. "The more upset you are, the faster the venom will work."

The head of the officer slumped to one side. The deputy doing the filming kept at it while the other asked, "He's not hurt, is he?"

"He fainted," said Bella. "He's not the first. Keep filming. You'll get a million hits on YouTube. If he croaks, he'll be the first man in history to die from the bite of a mechanical snake with rubber fangs. Look. It didn't even break the skin."

Steve leaned in Heather's direction. "It's time for us to leave."

Heather and Bella gathered what they intended to take and made for the door with Steve holding on to Heather's arm and Mike leading the way. The deputies, doubled over in laughter, didn't attempt to stop them.

Bella and Heather were still laughing as they closed their car doors. Bella said, "That's the best snake bite I've ever seen."

As their laughter died, the car became uncomfortably quiet. Steve broke the silence as he placed a hand on Bella's shoulder. "It's good to laugh, but it also helps to have a good cry."

Heather glanced to the right. A single tear made a path on Bella's cheek. Many more followed on the way home as she stroked Mike's head. Living with Blake

Brumley must have been hard. Yet, for good or bad, he'd been the only father Bella had any memory of. They'd shared experiences. That had to count for something. Steve had nailed it again. Bella needed to cry. Heather wanted to join her.

# CHAPTER 11

Steve had no more sat in his recliner than a cacophony of barks, hisses and high-pitched commands erupted from beyond the pet door. The flap of plastic in the cat door slapped open and shut. He heard what sounded like old-school metal track spikes skidding on porcelain tile. The cat's claws dug into the carpet as Max gained traction in the living room. Steve sighed. The meeting between Max and Mike had not gone well. He wondered if blood had been shed on Heather's side of the pet portal.

The voice of Bella came from the direction of the dining room as the pet door double-slapped again. "Mike! Don't go after that cat."

Too late. The jingle of Mike's vaccination and identification tags might as well have been a bell attached to a milk cow. At least he wouldn't be able to ambush Max. The sound of short inhales and exhales rose from Steve's ankles as Mike paused to sniff out the unfamiliar territory. A snort to clear the nose, and the dog jingled his way toward the bedrooms.

It didn't take long. A musical triplet of yelps came from Mike, "Yipe, yipe, yipe!" Doggie paws beat a fast retreat down the hall. Steve had no time to prepare. Eighteen pounds of cocker spaniel landed on his lap. Mike turned to face the hall, his whole body trembling under Steve's hands. The lapping sound of his tongue alternated with throaty baby-like cries.

Steve's front door swung open as if a police raid had been ordered. "Where's Mike? Is he hurt?" asked Bella.

Before Steve could answer, Mike had been lifted from his lap.

"He's bleeding." Bella spoke to the spaniel as if he were a baby, "Did that mean kitty hurt you?"

Heather joined in. "Poor thing. He'll be fine. It's only on his nose."

Bella continued consoling with the kind of babble people speak to injured children and pets.

Steve summarized the encounter. "Pecking order has been established. Max remains king of his two castles. They'll steer a wide path around each other for a while, and things will be fine."

Heather stroked the whimpering dog's head. "Why don't you take Mike next door? You two can get settled in, and I'll lock the pet door. Let's not have round two of a cat and dog fight tonight."

Steve had other things besides felines and K-9s on his mind. "Bella, what would you like for supper?"

The room remained silent, so Steve asked again.

"I get to choose?" asked Bella.

"You're our guest. What sounds good?" asked Heather.

"Are you sure you want me to decide?"

Steve noted the reticence in Bella's voice. Before his question about food, she had no trouble talking on an adult level. "You travel all over the world. I'm sure you have some favorites."

The springs in the couch beside Steve's recliner squeaked. Bella and Mike had settled themselves. Bella explained, "When we're at home, I can only eat meat from wild game. We have a cook that specializes in creating recipes for Blake's cookbooks. He comes in and makes a ton of dishes. I'm stuck with frozen heat-and-serve dinners. Some are all right, but others gross me out. Ever tried crow-k-bobs?"

"Can't say that I have," said Steve.

Bella kept talking. "When we traveled, Blake insisted on ordering the meals. For me, it was meat and salads. I had to stay at an exact weight so I'd look the same when we filmed. When I turned thirteen, he became a fanatic about how I looked."

Heather asked, "Do you think Blake had been getting you ready to model swimwear for a long time?"

Before Bella could answer, Steve interrupted. "What swimwear?"

Heather said, "That contract was one of the things we found in the safe. Blake was to get a cut of swimsuits sold, along with other compensations."

Bella said, "I wasn't allowed in the room if Blake was talking business, but I knew how to sneak around so I could hear him. He had a ten-year business plan that put me in skimpy outfits. He made a deal that put me fishing in exotic locations. I overheard him pitch it to a producer one night. He called it a fin-and-skin show. My skin, his show and he'd get the money."

"That explains the swimwear you were to model today," said Heather.

"Uh-huh. I did the photoshoots for the line in September. I hated it." Her voice lowered. "Do you think I'm weird for not wanting to wear a thong?"

Steve's stomach erupted in a sound that could best be described as other-worldly. "Before I perish, someone needs to order supper."

"How about pizza?" asked Heather. "Two large hand-tossed, one supreme and one pepperoni with extra cheese and a side order of breadsticks and marinara sauce."

"Yeah!" said Bella.

"Leave the armadillo off mine," said Steve.

Bella wasn't to be outdone. "Young armadillo isn't as bad as other things I've eaten. Cleaning them is the hard part."

Heather stepped into the kitchen to call in the order. She prepared a salad while Steve quizzed Bella on her world travels.

The doorbell interrupted their conversation. "After we eat I'd like to hear the story about Blake shooting Dart."

Steve and Bella joined Heather in the dining room. Bella didn't need to be asked twice to help herself to the pizza. Heather passed the salad to Bella. Swallowing a large bite of pizza, she said, "No thanks, I've had enough salad to last the rest of my life."

Heather smiled. "Well, I guess it won't hurt you to do without veggies one night."

Two slices of pizza remained, when Heather said, "Uh-oh, here comes Max out of Steve's bedroom. Bella, would you mind going next door to make sure the pet door is locked? I'd hate for Mike and Max to tangle again."

The front door to Steve's townhome clicked shut. The couch beside him gave a slight squeak. "What do you think?" asked Heather in a whisper.

Steve's head shook from side to side. "There are different types of exploitation. This one makes me sick. I see why Bella didn't like Blake. It makes me wonder how many others shared the same feelings."

"I agree. There may be a long line of people who wanted to see Blake dead. What about finding Bella's parents?"

"It'll be a needle in a haystack. We're going to have work harder than we ever have. Even if we succeed, we might bring more heartache to Bella if her parents don't want her."

# CHAPTER 12

Heather showed Bella to the spare bedroom in her townhome. "Change into pajamas if you want to get more comfortable."

Bella dumped the contents of her bag and backpack on the queen-size bed and began to hang articles of clothing in the closet. All the clothes she brought bore a camouflage pattern, except a single pair of thick brown hunting pants and some monotone socks.

Heather looked at the forest of items and asked, "Didn't you bring any normal clothes?"

Bella shrugged. "I'm supposed to get shorts, shirts, and tank tops for the fishing series, but our sponsor hasn't shipped them yet. Only the bathing suits I was supposed to model today." She looked at the pile. "The only clothes I can be seen in are what Blake contracted for me to wear. He was big into branding, and so are the people who sponsor our show."

"I've never seen so much camo."

Bella lifted a set of long-johns with a drop seat, examined it, and shook her head in disgust. "Everything has to have the manufacturer's logo on it, and I was taught to make sure the logo was prominently displayed." Her hand made a sweeping motion over the clothing on the bed. "Blake didn't want to take any chances of someone snapping a photo of me when I wasn't wearing something from one of his sponsors. He did the same thing. Ever seen a camo tux? The sponsor had one specially made for him."

Heather shook her head. The more Bella spoke of her life, the more she realized how controlling Blake Brumley had been. The thought of having to wear camo panties and bras sent a cringe down her spine.

How would Bella react to a taste of freedom? Time to find out. She went to her bedroom and fished out a tattered Princeton University sweatshirt and matching warm-up bottoms. She stepped into the guest bedroom and held up the jersey. "Would you like to wear these tonight?"

Bella's eyes opened wide. "Can I? These are so cool."

A camo shirt and pants Bella had come dressed in sailed across the room. Heather gasped. In front of her stood one of the most perfectly sculpted young women she'd ever seen. Her unbraided waist-length hair draped over the bra and panties, giving the teen a Lady Godiva look. Yet, this wasn't a woman on horseback with nothing but her locks to cover her. This was an excited teenage girl tugging on fleece bottoms that hit her mid-ankle. She squealed in delight as she shrugged into a simple sweatshirt with frayed cuffs.

"These are great. They're so soft." Bella sat on the edge of the queen bed and cast her gaze upward. "Ms. Heather, will you be honest with me?"

Heather didn't know what to make of the question. "I'll be as honest as I can."

Bella rolled her eyes. "That sounds like something a lawyer would say."

The air seemed to thicken. Heather knew Bella needed someone who could give her more than legal counsel. She needed a friend. What did she know about being a friend to a teenage girl?

"Ask your question," said Heather. "I'll do my best to give you an honest answer."

"What are the chances of you and Mr. Smiley finding my parents?"

Heather took in a full breath and released it through her teeth in a huff. "Not good."

"That's what I thought." Bella's gaze had dropped to her lap. "I hope that doesn't mean you won't try as hard as you can."

Heather sat beside her. "I give you my word, Steve and I will do what we can to find your birth parents. Steve is tenacious when he gets on a case." Heather took her hand. "But I can't promise we'll be successful. Also, I can't promise it will mean a happy ending if and when we do find your mom and dad."

Bella pursed her lips the way people do when they have a hard question to ask. She eased into the question. "I like Mr. Smiley a lot. I know he used to be a good detective."

"He was the top homicide detective in Houston."

Bella nodded and continued. "That was before he lost his sight. Do you think he's up to finding my parents?"

Heather thought of the best way to answer. "If my parents went missing, my first phone call would be to Steve Smiley. Don't worry about his blindness. That's where you and I can help him. He'll need full descriptions of what he can't see."

Bella smiled. "I like the idea of helping him." She paused. "Thanks for the talk. Gwen was the only woman I could talk to like this." Her face hardened. "Until Blake fired her."

Heather followed the thread. "Any idea why?"

Bella's head shook side to side. "That's the way he was. Big Blake did what he wanted, when he wanted, and to whoever he wanted."

The extent of the intended exploitation of Bella's body and soul hit Heather like a club. She could imagine future posters of Bella on the bedroom walls of teenage boys across the world. Blake Brumley, the master showman, had a gold mine on his hands.

People killed for goldmines.

Heather wanted to consult with Steve further, but that could wait until tomorrow. A full day awaited them, and an unpleasant conversation with Captain Charles Loving clawed at her mind.

# CHAPTER 13

Heather washed breakfast dishes as Steve sat in her recliner. It was a twin to the one in his townhome, but the fabric hadn't matched anything Heather's interior designer suggested. The designer remedied the problem by having the new chair reupholstered with the same material as Heather's couch. In Steve's opinion, she ruined it.

He ran his hand over the chair's arm. Changing the fabric from thick manly tweed to something soft and feminine spoiled a perfectly good recliner. Recliners are made for football games, watching the news, and naps. In his chair, he could yank on the wooden handle and settle in for a good movie. The recliner in Heather's townhome might as well have had a sign on it that read NO RECLINING.

He wasn't sure if Bella had recovered enough from her pizza binge to be much use in providing information. Given permission to eat her fill, she'd reached multiple times into the cardboard box. That hadn't stopped her from polishing off a full breakfast this morning. After which she flopped on the couch next to him and issued moans of contentment. Mike's name tags jingled as he bounded onto the couch. The jingling continued several more seconds. The dog must've made a lap or two before settling.

"Heather, are you ready to take notes?" he asked.

"Go ahead. I can hear."

"Bella," said Steve. "You've presented us with some difficult tasks. Unless I'm mistaken, you're more interested in finding your mom and dad than you are in finding Blake Brumley's killer. Am I right?"

"Uh-huh."

"This is where things get complicated. Most murders are committed by someone who knows the victim. Investigators start close and work their way out. Because you and Blake spent so much time together, that means the people who know you best will be the most likely ones to have shot Blake. They are also the ones that can give us information about how you came to Blake and Jolene."

Bella didn't sound convinced when she said, "Blake made tons of business deals. Some of them didn't work out. He wasn't always honest, and people got mad. It could have been one of those people."

Steve considered elevating his feet but didn't want to interrupt the contented atmosphere and Bella's willingness to talk. He kept his feet on the floor. "You're right. It could have been any number of people. We'll get to those later. For now, let's stick to the people who were closest to Blake."

He gave her a moment to take in what he'd said and to prepare for what was to come. "I don't want you to get upset, but I'm going to talk to you this morning like I'm a cop. Unless we have a witness or a confession, we start with the people closest to the victim. The police have a very unusual murder weapon and crime. I've never heard of anyone being shot with .416 Remington Magnum, especially at long range. Jolene Cox either owns or used to own a gun like that. She also knows better than anyone how you came to be adopted. Do you see how your adoption and the murder investigation overlap?"

"Yeah, but I don't think she had anything to do with killing Blake. She didn't dislike either of us enough to do something like that. She wanted to do her own thing."

"Did she and Blake ever fight? Did you hear either of them make threats?"

Bella took a moment before she answered. "It wasn't like that. Jolene focused on the hunts." She paused. "Is logistics the right word?"

Steve affirmed that it was and Bella continued. "Blake spent his time on show production, marketing and sales."

Heather moved to the couch. "Young lady, you don't look too good."

"I'm stuffed like a tube of deer sausage."

"Overstuffed, I'm guessing," said Steve. "Tell us about Blake shooting Dart."

"Oh, that. It was nothing." The couch made a crunching, popping sound as Bella sat. "Do I have to tell the whole story?"

"I'd like to know what Blake shot him with and why."

"A Browning twelve gauge, but the shell didn't have any pellets."

The silence that followed told Steve Heather hadn't heard of a shot-less shotgun shell either.

"A shotgun shell with no pellets? Why would he have something like that?" Steve asked.

"Blake was lousy with a shotgun. We went to more countries than I can remember. Some of the episodes showed us shooting game birds. If you watch the show, you'll never see Blake in the picture with a bird falling after he shot."

She paused. "Sorry. I didn't mean to tell Steve to watch the show."

"Don't worry about that. Talk to me like I can see."

"Anyway, they'd show him shooting from a side angle. He'd shoot his gun, but his shells didn't have any shot. They look the same, kick about the same, and are as loud. But the only thing that comes out of the barrel is the plastic wad that separates the powder from where the shot should be. They'd edit in a bird falling someone else had shot."

Heather spoke before Steve had a chance to. "Are you saying Blake shot Dart with a piece of plastic?"

Bella nodded. "It was this past summer, and Dart had on a t-shirt. Blake drilled him square in the back from about eight yards away. It must have stung like a yellow jacket."

Steve said, "You told us yesterday Dart was your kind-of boyfriend. How did he get that close to you if Blake was so protective? Surely, he didn't want any boys coming around."

Bella looked at Steve. "I met Dart at the pet store where Gwen and I took Mike for a bath and nail trim."

Steve interrupted. "The same pet store the shot came from yesterday?"

"Same one. We kind of hit it off. I didn't expect him to visit me at home. Blake was so mad at Gwen."

"Is that when he fired her?"

"No, that came later. Gwen didn't know Dart would show up, either. I don't know why he fired her."

"Heather," said Steve. "We need to plan a trip to the pet store and have a talk with Mr. Dart. I'm going next door while you get ready. That is unless you're planning on wearing your robe and house shoes on our stops today."

The couch beside Steve squeaked. "How did you know what she was wearing?" asked Bella.

"I know the scuffing sound of her house shoes. That told me she wasn't barefoot or wearing street shoes or boots. Her robe makes a rustling sound against the fancy nighties she wears. Also, she hasn't put on fresh perfume yet."

"Wow! You can tell all that?" A short pause preceded an excited voice. "What am I wearing?"

Steve rose from the chair and spoke as he walked. "Something soft and stretchy. Between last night's pizza and this morning's breakfast I'm not sure you can get into your regular clothes."

# CHAPTER 14

Max jumped onto the arm of Steve's chair and snuggled down on his lap. Steve rubbed the cat's head and listened to his purr. A visual image of Blake shooting Dart coursed through his mind. "It was a good thing Blake couldn't hit anything but air with a shotgun, wasn't it, Max?"

The knock on the front door interrupted his musings. From his chair, Steve hollered, "Come in."

The front door opened and chilly air filtered in along with the footsteps of two people.

"Who's with you, Bella?"

"How did you know someone was with me?"

"Soft footsteps, and you don't wear perfume. It's not Heather's brand, but it's very familiar."

The fragrance arrested him and took him back in time. Maggie had a ritual she performed when spraying on that particular scent. She'd give a short squirt to each wrist, and she'd mist the air in front of her, close her eyes, and walk through the cloud. Her shoulder-length blonde hair became infused with a smell that reminded him of honeysuckle and spring. It never overpowered or had that too-sweet smell like the fog following his Aunt Flora.

Maggie said it wasn't the perfume, but the person's body chemistry mixing with the fragrance that produced the unique scent of a woman. Whoever had walked into his townhome had similar body chemistry to Maggie's. He swallowed hard.

Bella said, "Steve, this is Gwen Fontaine, my former nanny. She called this morning and came to see me. Heather said she needed to finish getting ready, so I thought I'd bring Gwen over and introduce you."

Steve rose from his chair and held out a hand. A slim hand took his. It felt eerily similar to the one he'd held for years. The fragrance of his late wife cascaded over him. He choked out a "Nice to meet you, Ms. Fontaine. Please come in and make yourself comfortable."

"Thank you, Mr. Smiley. Bella's told me so much about you in the last half hour. I feel like I've known you for years."

Steve had to turn away. Gwen's voice had a soft, floating quality to it. It wasn't Maggie's voice, but it appealed to his sensitive hearing. It matched the perfume in its ability to stir something he'd buried years ago. He chastised himself silently.

Gwen rested a hand on his shoulder. Her voice drifted onto him, "I hope you don't mind us barging in, Steve. Is it all right if I call you Steve?"

She used his first name as if she'd said it a thousand times. His hand moved to cover Gwen's out of some dormant instinct. He caught himself and lowered it.

"I'm not one to stand on formality, Gwen. Especially when I'm sitting in my recliner with house shoes on." He issued a smile and realized how wide it must appear.

It was time to change the subject. "How did you hear Bella was staying with Heather?"

"Olin Field told me. He thought Bella might need a shoulder to cry on or at least someone to talk to. After watching her grow up and globe-trotting with her, I feel more like an aunt than her teacher."

"Uncle Olin and Aunt Gwen," said Steve. "Is that what they were to you, Bella?"

"I don't call Gwen my aunt, but she's been there for me when I didn't have anyone else." A hard edge of an offended teenage girl came to her voice. "That is until Blake fired her. He fired Uncle Olin, too."

Steve resettled himself in his chair. "Gwen, if the police investigation drags on, there's a good chance they'll want to question you."

"Why?"

Naiveté flavored her question. "It's no big deal," said Steve. "They'll know today Blake fired you. That's not much of a motive, but they need to be thorough."

"How will the police know Blake fired me?"

"Bella will tell them. We're to meet with the police this afternoon."

81

"Do you want me to go with Bella?" asked Gwen.

Steve shook his head. "That's not the way they work. Before they call you in, they'll do a background check on you."

Wariness crept into her voice.

"Should I hire an attorney?"

"Don't worry. The first time around they won't be thorough. Police look for prior arrests and check to see if you have any outstanding warrants. If they find anything that causes them to raise an eyebrow they'll ask you about it. Otherwise, they'll want to know where you were at the time of the shooting. If you have a solid alibi, they shouldn't bother you again. I doubt there'll be a second interview."

"As long as high school speeding tickets don't make me a criminal, there shouldn't be a second interview."

Gwen's voice had a soft, playful quality about it. It reminded him of a song that had been popular a long time before Maggie came into his life. He had to shake off the memory before he could continue.

"You're right," said Steve. "There probably won't be a second interview. Not unless they see something out of the ordinary."

Gwen's laugh had an effervescent quality to it. Not the silly bubbles of youth, more like a glass of well-aged wine. She said, "I was four and a half hours west of here in Fredericksburg doing early Christmas shopping on the day Blake was shot."

"That's far enough for any cop." He shifted in his chair. "You don't have much of a Texas accent. Where are you from?"

"Miami. Sun and sand."

"Were you living there when Blake hired you to take care of Bella?"

"I taught school right up the interstate in Huntsville. My marriage fell apart, and I needed a fresh start. I didn't plan on staying so long, but I fell in love with Bella and couldn't stand to leave her."

The front door opened and in rushed the smell of Heather's perfume and pine trees. She swept into the room and asked, "Ready to go?"

"Do I have to?" asked Bella. "Can't I stay here with Gwen?"

Heather seemed to be waiting on Steve to say something. She killed time by saying, "I don't know."

"I think that's a wonderful idea," said Steve. "Heather and I need to discuss some things in private. This will give you two a chance to catch up. We could all grab a late lunch when we get back." He paused. "That is, if you'd like to, Gwen."

"I'd love to. My day is free."

"Great. It's a date."

Steve hadn't meant to sound so enthusiastic, and he certainly hadn't intended to use the word *date*. Heather didn't miss much. He had no doubt she'd raised at least one eyebrow and possibly two. He'd find out soon enough. They stepped out the door and into the brisk

morning breeze, on their way to the pet store to interview
Dart Salinsky.

# CHAPTER 15

The pet store showed no sign of the previous day's invasion by police. Zoo-like smells assaulted Heather as soon as the front door closed behind them. Puppies yapped in the distance, and a bird of unknown plumage let out a call that sounded like a cry for freedom. A sign on a far wall read *Doggie Day Spa*. She headed that direction but was stopped by a perky worker with half her hair dyed red and the other half green. Earrings in the likeness of a Christmas tree hung from each ear.

"Can I help you?" she asked with a voice that sounded supercharged by energy drinks.

"Do you know if Dart Salinsky is working today?" asked Heather.

"For sure. You can find Dart giving Betty her treatment. Dart is so good with her, and he's so committed and so passionate about his work. They tried to promote him to assistant manager, but he so wouldn't have it."

"Were you working yesterday?" Heather asked.

"Part of the day." The girl tilted her head. "Why all the questions? Are you with the police? I answered your questions yesterday."

"We're private investigators. Did it surprise you the police handcuffed Dart?" asked Steve.

She flipped a wrist downward to dismiss the question. "No. Dart talks about all the times he's been arrested for the cause. He's so cool."

"What cause?"

"I probably should have said causes. He's so involved in everything related to animals."

"Did they take anyone else in for questioning?"

The girl brought a hand to the green hair hanging down the left side of her face and began to form a curl around her index finger. "Nooo…not that I saw."

"What about the manager on duty?"

"Oh, neither one of them were here. But Dart was. He's like the unofficial manager. Know what I mean?"

Steve shook his head. "I'm old. You'll need to explain it to me."

"It's like he wears an invisible superhero suit or something. He walks by, and it's like he sees everything. He's worked here so long he knows more than the manager and the assistant managers. They even let him open and close the store."

"They let him have keys to the store?" asked Heather.

"For sure."

86

The store's intercom overrode a Christmas carol featuring dogs barking a melody. "Attention associates. If you're not currently assisting a customer, report to the kittens. Code 14."

"Got to go," said the young woman. "Somebody didn't latch the gate. We'll have kittens all over the store if we don't hurry." She pointed to a blinking neon sign identifying the location of pooch pampering. "You'll find Dart there. He'll be up to his elbows with a pug. She's a regular customer."

Heather saw a young man hunched over a deep sink, having a one-sided conversation with a tan pug. If she hadn't known better, she would have thought he was talking to another person. "Excuse me."

The young man glanced up. "Be with you in a few minutes." He returned to scrubbing out the clefts in fur and talking to the dog. After rinsing, the pug shook, sprayed water across an enclosed area, and sneezed. "Bless you, Betty," said the man. He wrapped a towel around broad hips and shoulders and rubbed with vigor. He hefted her onto a table equipped with a hairdryer.

Heather watched in silence as he continued his dog spa treatment. Pinned on an apron awash in a sea of animal rights and preservation buttons was a name tag reading DART. Interspersed were slogan buttons that read: *Eat a Hunter—Tastes Like Chicken, Vegetarians Save Lives,* and *Don't Kill Anything With a Face.*

The hairdryer covered any chance of conversing with Dart, so Heather pulled Steve to a spot a few yards away. "He's tall, skinny and looks to be about twenty-five years old. He has black hair pulled up in a man-bun. The ink on his arm is pictures of dogs. He's wearing an apron with every animal rights organization and anti-hunting and anti-fishing slogan you can imagine. It's easy to see what the girl was talking about with his causes."

Steve nodded but said nothing.

The pampered pug rolled over, exposing a pink belly. With front paws curled inward, she wiggled into the towel and closed her eyes. The K-9 version of a chin to tail massage began amid moans of dog ecstasy. The man finally turned his head their way. "Whisper. Betty doesn't like to have her massage interrupted."

Heather searched for something appropriate to say that would balance her lack of concern for an over-indulged pooch while not sounding uncaring. Nothing came to mind. Thankfully, Steve came to the rescue as he whispered, "We won't take much of your time. We wanted to let you know how Mike's doing."

"Mike?"

"He's one of your former clients, a three-year-old cocker spaniel. His caregiver is Bella Brumley. She told us she used to bring Mike to you for your special touch."

Dart's head jerked up. His eyes flared in alarm as he interrupted. "What did they do to him?"

Steve held out an open palm. "Mike's fine. So is Bella."

Betty, the pug, opened her eyes and issued a low growl.

"Sorry, dear. These people were telling me about Mike. You remember Mike. He's the dapper spaniel, the color of a penny."

The dog let out a huff that caused her jowls to flutter. Betty rolled over on her stomach and turned her head away.

Dart continued the massage. After Betty began to snore, he asked, "Is Mike still in that haunted house?"

"He's at our townhomes along with Bella," said Steve. "We have a pet door that connects our two dining rooms. Mike and Heather's companion, a feline Maine Coon named Max, can come and go as they please."

Dart kept rubbing Betty but gave Heather a nod of approval. "That's an interesting arrangement. You don't find many people who are willing to share their children. Did Mike and Max have any trouble adjusting?"

"Max is older and has lived with me for years," said Heather. "He wasn't keen on the newcomer invading his space and set his boundaries last night when Bella and Mike moved in. We've locked the pet door, but plan on gradually getting them together. Any suggestions?"

"Hmmm. Spaniels tend to be protective and territorial. Let them get used to being around each other gradually. I'd try an hour a day under strict supervision for the next few days. Give them time, and they'll become lifelong companions."

"Thanks," said Steve. "That's great advice."

Steve took his time when conducting interviews. He waited until Dart's curiosity got the best of him.

"How did you two get involved with Mike and Bella?"

Heather placed a business card on the table where Dart could read it without interrupting Betty's massage. "We happened to be walking into the mall yesterday when Blake Brumley was killed. We took Bella under our wings. She wants us to find her birth-mother and father."

Steve broke in. "We spoke with a store employee when we walked in. She said the police had you in handcuffs and took you to the office for a long time yesterday. Is that true?"

He nodded. "I guess they didn't like my attitude when I found out who was shot." He looked at Betty. "I shouldn't have celebrated like I did, but Blake Brumley was a mass murderer. He raised a nice girl to become a killer like him. Can you believe what some parents do to their kids?"

Steve didn't respond to the question. "That's not the only reason the cops came down on you, was it?"

"What do you mean?"

"We did some checking before we came today. You have quite a record of arrests for such a young man."

A look of self-righteousness filled his face. "Someone has to protect animals, and I'm willing to go out on a limb to draw attention to the cause. If that means getting arrested to save lives, so be it."

Steve nodded his head. As he was apt to do, he immediately shifted to another subject. "Bella told us

Blake shot you when you came to their home. The cops questioned you about that, didn't they?"

"You sound like a cop."

"Used to be. So did Ms. McBlythe." Steve kept going. "You must have filed a report on Blake for shooting you."

A huff of exasperation came from Dart. "That was a waste of time. They told me I was lucky they didn't charge me with attempted burglary. Bella invited me inside. Of course, Blake said she didn't. They took his word for it and never talked to Bella."

"Did you go out to see Bella often?"

"Bella? You think I went there for her? No way. I went to convince Bella she needed to let me find a proper home for Mike. I couldn't talk about it here at work. The manager is lenient with me, but that would be over the line."

"Ahh," said Steve. "So you and Bella weren't romantically involved?"

His head shook with fervor. "There's no denying she's a hot girl, but she's a serial killer." He paused and issued a look that asked for understanding. "I felt sorry for her. I thought her dad exploited her." His tone hardened. "That doesn't change the fact she has innocent blood on her hands." He stole a glance at Heather. "I have a reputation to maintain."

"What did you think when the cops found a .416 Remington Magnum from the roof?"

A blank look crossed Dart's thin, bearded face. "I assume you're talking about a type of rifle."

"Ever shot a rifle?" asked Steve.

Dart's head shook from side to side. "Two people asked me that same question yesterday: a cop and a TV reporter. The answer's still no. The only reason people own a gun is to kill living creatures."

"You must have talked to the same reporter who tried to interview us," said Heather.

"If she's short, good looking and had a guy filming her, I did. She was here in the store interviewing me again today. Her name is Alexandria. I didn't catch the last name."

Steve lifted his chin. "They were here yesterday and today?"

Betty yawned and rose to her feet. She extended her front paws, stretching her back. She looked at Dart and seemed to smile with her eyes.

Dart bent over to receive a lick on his cheek. "Is that all the questions you have? I need to take care of Betty's nails." He looked at the pug. "We have so much to catch up on, don't we Betty?"

Heather wanted to know more about the reporter, but she couldn't formulate a relevant question before Steve said, "That's all for now. We may have more questions for you later. How can we get in touch with you?"

"My card is on the counter. It has my e-mail and cell number on it." He stroked Betty's head and said,

"You seem like you could use a companion, Mr. Smiley. Mike has a great disposition."

"He already has a caregiver," said Steve.

"So did Betty until her first family adopted a boy who was allergic to dogs. I found out her original family was sending her to the county animal shelter." He looked into Betty's eyes. "I found my favorite girl a nice safe home, didn't I?"

Dart focused on the pedicure while Steve turned toward the front door. With no sign of stray kittens seeking an escape into the parking lot, the duo made for the car. Heather started the engine to the Lexus, called Bella's cell phone and told her the restaurant where she and Gwen needed to meet them.

# CHAPTER 16

Seat belts unlatched at the same time. Heather stole a glance at Steve. In winter he preferred dark trousers and a medium weight all-weather jacket. A white t-shirt peeked out of the neck of a long sleeve blue shirt. The only variation to his wardrobe on most days was the shirt's color. If he felt really adventurous, or if the weather turned cold, he'd cover the shirt with a sweater. Today he grabbed his gray wool scarf to ward off the residual effects of the previous day's blustery wind.

As soon as they stepped into the vestibule of the restaurant, Steve dragged a pocket comb from an inside pocket of his jacket. "How does my hair look?"

Heather couldn't believe it. She usually had to remind him to comb his brown mop. Of course, today was different. They were to meet someone who sounded as good as she smelled.

"It looks good enough to go to the prom," she said.

He grumbled out something not worth repeating. They secured a booth and ordered hot tea while Steve drummed his fingers on the table.

Gwen and Bella approached. "I hope we haven't kept you waiting," said Gwen.

After exchanging pleasantries, Bella slid into the booth beside Heather. Gwen gave Bella a sideways glance and took her place beside Steve.

The waitress arrived to take drink orders for the new arrivals and left menus.

Gwen caught Bella's gaze. A nudge of her head to one side gave the unspoken signal for the two to go to the restroom. Bella nodded. Gwen slid out of the booth and said, "If you'll excuse me, I need to powder my nose. We left in a bit of a hurry."

Bella rose from her seat. "Me too. I'll go with you."

"What does she look like?" asked Steve when they were out of earshot.

"Who?" Heather bit her tongue to keep a snicker from escaping. His interest in Bella's former nanny surprised her. Devotion to Maggie had been an impenetrable wall. Were cracks beginning to appear?

"Since I know you have auburn hair that comes down below your shoulders, green eyes, you're five-foot-six-inches tall, and you weigh—"

Heather didn't let him finish. "Don't say it. Talking about a woman's weight at any time between Thanksgiving and the last day of January is forbidden. I insist on having a chance to enjoy the holidays and to work off seasonal gorging."

The corners of his mouth pulled up. Heather placed her hands in her lap. "Since I've already described Bella to you, I'm assuming you mean Gwen Fontaine."

He nodded.

She didn't tease Steve often, mainly because they went days with little or no interaction. Today, however, she saw her opening and took it. "She's quite attractive except for her ears."

"Ears?"

"Oh, it's nothing. The holes from the gauges can be fixed by a skilled plastic surgeon."

"Uh-huh."

"And her bangs hide the tattoo on her forehead. I do wonder who Willie Ray might be."

Steve turned away from her and shook his head. "You need lessons in lying. The key to a believable lie is grounding it in truth. If you'd told me her hair was raven black with a few strands of silver, I'd have believed it."

Heather's mouth hung open. "How did you know what her hair looks like?"

"I didn't, but I had a clue or two. Gwen's voice has the last remnants of an accent that sounds far-eastern. I'm guessing she's third-generation American and her grandmother was a war bride or came over with her family in the mid part of the twentieth century. Gwen told me she taught school after graduating from college. She also said she's divorced. If teaching public school doesn't give you gray hair, a divorce will. I'd say she's early-to-mid forties, evenly built and weighs about one hundred thirty pounds."

Heather shook her head in disbelief. "How did you guess her weight?"

"I listened when she sat on my couch. She sat on the cushion nearest my chair. The spring under that particular cushion makes a little squeak at one hundred and twenty-five pounds or if someone plops down. She doesn't impress me as being a plopper. The spring squeaked a little, but not much. I split the difference between one hundred and twenty-five pounds and one forty-five."

Heather knew when she was beaten. "Gwen is attractive, but not flashy. Her complexion is olive. You're right about the Asian ancestry. I'd say only one part in four. She has dark eyes. Makeup is minimal, but she doesn't need much. Unobtrusive laugh lines crinkle around the eyes, but not any more than I'd expect from a woman her age. I didn't notice any mid-life plastic surgery or scars of any kind."

Steve issued another "Uh-huh," and asked, "Can you describe the laugh lines in more detail?"

"What do you mean?"

"Are they noticeably white against her olive skin?"

"I don't know. I didn't look that close." Heather stole another glance. "Why is that important?"

"It's not, but white laugh-lines around the eyes can give you an indication of how much time a person spends in bright sunlight."

Heather shook her head. Twenty-six years of being a cop had trained Steve to notice the smallest details. She'd have to pay more attention.

Heather silently contemplated her partner while she sipped her tea. Was Steve thinking about the young man at the pet store? It seemed more likely his thoughts were on the handsome woman that expressed such joy at being reunited with Bella. Could the pain of losing Maggie finally subside enough for him to notice another woman?

Her musings were cut short when Bella slid into the booth beside her. Conversation bounced across the table like a game of tennis. Steve's countenance brightened with each passing moment. Heather enjoyed seeing Steve interact with a woman. There was a boy-like charm about him.

Bella looked at the menu with wide eyes. "You have no idea how nice it is to eat something I didn't have to pluck, skin, or scrape scales off of."

Steve and Gwen sat with not much distance between them. Heather tilted her head. The sight of the two of them laughing seemed right, and wrong, at the same time. Her emotions began a playful wrestling match, like two kittens boxing with paws, not claws. His interest in this woman with a silk voice couldn't be denied. Yet, he'd sworn his deceased wife would be the only woman who ever had, or would, win his heart.

Another emotion occurred to her. Was that a touch of jealousy she felt in the pit of her stomach?

Heather's self-examination and ponderings ended when the server arrived to take their orders. She followed Gwen's lead and ordered a salad while Bella ordered beer-battered cod and French fries. Steve, a creature of habit, chose chicken-fried steak, signature mashed garlic potatoes, and a vegetable medley. He asked that the steak be cut in bite-sized pieces in the kitchen. As he began to tuck the cloth napkin under his chin, Gwen reached in, eager to help.

Bella chuckled.

"What's so funny?" asked Steve.

"You two look like you might want to have this booth to yourselves."

Gwen came to Steve's rescue. "I had some experience with a blind student a long time ago. I told you about him. Don't you remember?"

Bella hesitated. "Are you sure you told me about that? How old was I?"

"Apparently, you weren't old enough to remember."

"No matter," said Steve. "I'll take all the help I can get. Heather says I wear as much food as I eat." Steve reached for a glass of water. "By the way, Bella, we talked to Dart this morning."

Heather looked for a reaction. Gwen's eyebrows lifted as she buttered a roll. Bella leaned forward. "Did he ask about me?"

"He seemed glad to know both you and Mike were okay," said Steve, dodging half the question. "We heard the police got a little rough with him yesterday."

"Did they hurt him?"

"He's fine. He was elbow-deep in a sink giving a pug named Betty the full treatment."

Heather broke in. "He was reaching for red fingernail polish when we left."

Bella shook her head. "He's so good with dogs. Mike loves him."

A dropped tray shattered glasses and plates on the concrete floor near their booth. Wait staff sprang into action but not before a young waitress burst into tears. She strained to bend over a baby-bump and pick up the pieces of glass and crockery.

A scowling middle-aged woman with *Asst. Manager* embroidered on her shirt stormed across the room. Her words of chastisement came out as sharp as the shards of glass and carried to the far corners of the restaurant. "Becky, this will come out of your check."

Steve pulled a wad of bills in a money clip from his trousers and handed it to Heather. "Take care of this."

"You rat," said Heather. "You beat me to it again."

Heather stood, caught the attention of the woman standing guard over the waitress, and summoned her with a crooked finger. The woman came with an apology paving her way.

Heather held up a hand for the woman to stop talking. She peeled off a hundred dollar bill and handed it to the woman. "I know what the company pays for plates and glasses. This will cover the cost of the breakage."

The woman stared at her wide-eyed and said, "Keep your money, ma'am. Becky has to learn to be more careful. I'm taking the breakage out of her paycheck."

Heather dug in her purse, pulled out a business card and three hundred more dollars. "No matter what lessons we may need to learn, sometimes we all just need a little extra help. I'd like to speak to her, please."

The woman turned to the distraught waitress. "Becky, come here."

The young woman approached them, lips quivering. "Yes, ma'am?"

Heather handed the girl the bills. "This is for you and your baby. You look like you could use an early Christmas present."

The waitress looked at the money as if a bank vault had been opened to her. Her tears flowed afresh. "I can't believe it. Thank you. You don't know what this means to me."

Gwen rose and put her arm around the young waitress's shoulders. She looked at the assistant manager. "Do you mind if I take Becky to the restroom and help her get cleaned up?"

"Uhh...I guess not."

Heather turned an icy gaze to the assistant manager. "Do you know the name of the parent company of this restaurant?"

"Uhh."

"It's McBlythe Enterprises," said Heather. She held out a card. "Take a good look at my business card. You'll see my name is Heather McBlythe." She waited for the light to come on behind the woman's eyes.

Heather leaned in and whispered, "I suggest the next time one of the staff has an accident you grab a broom, dustpan, mop or whatever you need to get the mess cleaned up as quickly and quietly as possible. It's company policy that unintentional breakage is not to be passed on to the servers. I know. I helped write the policy."

Heather waved a hand at the crowd. "Look around you. This restaurant is filled with people who came to enjoy a good meal and to be served by people who care about them and act as a team. Tell the manager I'll stop in to see him soon."

The card quivered in the woman's hand as she left the table.

Heather slid into the booth and watched the assistant manager begin to sweep up the broken mess. She passed Steve's money clip back to him and said, "I believe we were talking about Dart when we were interrupted."

# CHAPTER 17

Bella locked her gaze on Heather. "Did you give the waitress that dropped the tray a bunch of money?"

Heather shrugged. "It's something of a game Steve and I play. If we come across someone in a jam, we try to help." Heather patted Bella on her arm. "You're going to be coming into some substantial money. Learn to be generous with it."

"Let's talk about Dart," said Steve.

Bella smoothed the napkin on her lap. "I'm surprised Dart isn't in jail. He told me about some of the times he'd been arrested. He also said he'd like to kill Blake."

"When did he say that?" asked Heather.

"The day Blake shot him."

Steve said, "If the police ask you about that, you'll need to tell them what you heard."

"Do I have to?"

"You need to answer truthfully," said Heather. "I'll be with you and make sure their questions stay on track."

Gwen returned to the table at the same time their food arrived. She went to work arranging Steve's plate. "You have half a buttered roll in front of you."

"Thank you. I could get used to pampering like this." He took a bite and released a soft moan. After he swallowed, he said, "Bella, remember the TV crew from yesterday?"

"Uh-huh."

"The police will ask you if you called them ahead of time and told them to be close by."

Gwen gave a quick twist of her head. "Why would they do that?"

"I'll let Heather explain." He lifted the roll and took another bite.

Heather looked around to make sure no eavesdroppers had joined the conversation. She leaned forward and motioned with her head for Gwen and Bella to do the same. "Bella said some pretty strong things about Blake on social media. When they find out someone alerted a news crew to be there to cover the story, they'll need to rule her out as a suspect."

Gwen reacted first. Her voice rose, and her words came sharp and quick. "I know Bella as well as any mother knows her child. She'd never do anything like that. She's a sweet girl who had to live with a self-indulgent monster."

Steve reached for Gwen's hand. He found it, but she jerked it away. He turned his head to her. "There's no need to get upset. We know Bella had nothing to do with

104

it. We're preparing her for what will come later on today."

Gwen righted her emotional ship. "I'm sorry. I guess I'm overprotective of Bella."

"Perfectly understandable," said Steve. "You got a bum deal when Blake let you go. He must have blamed you for Dart coming to see Bella."

Her head hung, and she nodded. "He had to blame someone. I guess it was my turn."

"Did he fire many people?" asked Steve.

Bella spoke with her mouth half-full of fish. "He did it all the time. He fired Uncle Olin, Gwen, our cooks, maids, yard workers, and anyone on the production team that questioned him. Heck, in a way, he fired his wife, Jolene."

"Speaking of Jolene," said Heather as she looked at Bella. "Did she get in contact with you yet?"

"Yeah, she called this morning from Canada."

Gwen's eyes opened wide. "Canada? How long has she been in Canada? What did she say?"

"Not much. I told Jolene I had everything under control and she didn't need to cut the hunt short."

"When did she arrive in Canada?" asked Steve.

"She left out of Houston yesterday afternoon. She flew to Quebec, spent the night, and took another plane north this morning."

Heather didn't need to look at Steve to know what he was thinking. Houston's Bush International Airport sat in far north Harris County, only a short drive from the pet store. Jolene Cox had plenty of time to fire the shot from the roof of the pet store, climb in a car, and scoot to the airport to catch her flight. If she carried a rifle case and ammunition with her, she had a built-in excuse if a dog alerted on her for gunshot residue.

The meal wound down, and Heather checked the time on her phone. Captain Loving's office would be their next stop. The name of the reporter flashed into her mind. Alexandria Ramos, AKA Alex Ramos, AKA boyfriend kisser. She would be a topic of conversation. The salad did a somersault in her stomach.

# CHAPTER 18

Steve unwound the scarf from his neck as Heather watched him in the rearview mirror. Bella filled her ears with white buds attached to wires that snaked down to her cell phone. They had all bid goodbye to Gwen. The next stop would be the building in Conroe that housed the office of Captain Charles Loving.

Heather had been rendered mute since the name of the woman reporter made its uninvited appearance in her mind. The memory of the kiss she'd witnessed the day before played as if on a loop. Steve pulled his cell phone out of his pocket and gave it a voice command to call Leo Vega, his former partner in homicide. He told it to go on speaker so Heather could hear. Heather glanced at his reflection in the mirror. Why was he calling Leo?

"Hey, partner, how's it going?" asked Steve.

"The usual for this time of year. People are celebrating the holidays by killing each other. Besides that, my children believe I have carte blanche with Santa. They gave me their Christmas wish-lists. I may have to rob a bank." He paused. "What kind of quasi-legal help do you need from me? I know it has something to do with the mall shooting."

"What makes you say that?"

"You're the celebrity-du-jour in homicide. We must have played the TV footage from last night's news a dozen times."

"Funny you should mention that."

"Uh-oh. Here it comes. I knew you called to ask a favor. Come on, out with it."

"You know me too well." Steve shifted in his seat. "I need you to contact the guy that shot the footage you've been watching. He and the reporter happened to be at the pet store filming some sort of pre-Christmas fluff piece. They finished a short time before Blake Brumley was murdered. They happened to be driving to the front entrance of the mall when the shot was fired."

Heather gasped. She hadn't recognized the significance of the timing of the interview and the appearance of the television truck. Did the reporter know ahead of time that something big was going to take place? Could she have prevented it? Another thought streaked across her mind. Was the reporter ambitious enough to be involved in a plot to kill Blake Brumley? It wouldn't be the first time a newsperson manufactured a story to promote their career. She wondered if her imagination had run completely away with her.

"When do you need the information?" asked Leo.

"Heather's representing Bella Brumley. The three of us have an appointment at the Sheriff's office this afternoon. We're on our way."

"That's not much time," said Leo.

"All I need you to do is call the manager of the TV station. Ask if they received a tip about a big story. I want to know how he reacts."

"Montgomery County S.O. isn't going to like me sticking my rather handsome nose in their investigation uninvited."

"I'd do it myself if I had the right kind of badge. Run it by Lieutenant Morgan. If he says no, forget it."

"I'll ask after I do it. Let's see what I can find out and get back to you."

"Thanks, Leo. Give my best to the family." Steve spoke the next words quickly. "Say, Leo, when did you get a nose job? The way I remember it, that proboscis of yours wouldn't look good on a camel."

Steve's phone went dead.

Heather realized she'd missed a turn. She made the block and waited at a stoplight. "Do you think Alexandria had something to do with the murder?"

"It's possible. It could also mean someone wanted this story covered as it unfolded. What doesn't make sense is why a TV reporter would drive to The Woodlands to interview a guy washing dogs when Houston has plenty of pet stores. That guy happens to be one of the biggest animal rights activists in the area and has at least one good reason to kill Blake Brumley.

Getting shot in the back with a shotgun tends to bring out the worst in people. It doesn't matter that it was a piece of plastic that hit him; it was the intention behind the action that could have caused Dart to seek revenge."

Heather put the pieces together in her mind. "Are you convinced someone called the reporter and told her where to show up and when?"

Steve gave his head a nod. "That's the way I see it."

Heather thought for a moment. "Do you think it was Dart?"

"The cops were quick to cuff him and drag him over the coals. From what he said about standing up for animals and what you said about the buttons on his vest, he's not opposed to publicity. I'm surprised they didn't take him in."

"With his arrest record, that would only be another button on his apron," said Heather.

A block passed in silence. Steve broke the silence. "As to why the police didn't haul him in, I believe they didn't want to give him the satisfaction of getting more publicity."

Heather nodded. It made sense. Besides, the only person they would be talking to would be his lawyer.

Steve turned to face her. "If you've finished going the wrong direction, let's go to Conroe. Captain Loving should be ready for us."

How did he know she'd missed a turn?

# CHAPTER 19

They headed north on I-45. Heather's thoughts turned to the coincidental leaving the country by Jolene Cox-Brumley. She had some explaining to do when she returned from the frozen north.

A mechanical voice came from Steve's phone announcing a call from Leo Vega.

"Sorry, Steve," said Leo. "I didn't get to the reporter or cameraman in time. The TV station manager told me he sent them to the mall and pet store to do a follow-up story. He also said they were asked to come to the sheriff's office after they finished."

"What about yesterday? Did the manager give you a hint as to how Alexandria Ramos knew where to be?"

"He closed tighter than an oyster. I cut him off when he started lecturing me on confidential sources."

"Thanks, Leo. Did you ask if the station was sending an attorney with them?"

"She's traveling separately and will meet them at the Sheriff's office."

"Good work, Leo. We may have more favors to ask before we get this sorted out."

The car remained quiet for a couple of miles. Steve leaned toward Heather. "What do you think?"

"It heightens my suspicion that Ms. Alexandria Ramos received advance notice to come to the pet store and be hanging around the mall. I'm wondering how much she knew ahead of time."

"I'm asking myself the same thing. Why else would the station be sending an attorney? They want to make sure their cub reporter doesn't say too much and give the station a black eye."

Bella's earbuds sat in her lap. "If Alexandria knew something was going to happen, could she be in trouble for not telling the cops?"

A pair of motorcycles with straight pipes made a slow pass of Heather's SUV. Despite the quality construction of the Lexus, the answer had to wait until they thundered well ahead.

"It's a gray area in the law," said Heather. "It depends on how much the reporter was told. The courts have to balance freedom of the press with the needs of the police to solve and sometimes prevent crimes. They usually give the nod to the press."

Steve added, "There's also the issue of public perception. People tend to react unfavorably if a reporter knows murder is going to be committed and doesn't say anything to prevent it."

Bella sat in silence, but not for long. "Blake said bad publicity is better than none. He was all about keeping our name in front of people. Do you think Alexandria Ramos knew what was going to happen?"

"You have the makings of a detective," said Steve. "I think Ms. Ramos will be asked some hard questions today."

Bella turned in her seat. "You didn't know until you talked to Dart about her coming to the pet store, did you?"

"Nope."

"Do you think the police know?"

Heather answered before Steve could. "If they don't, they will as soon as we tell them."

Steve unhooked his seat belt and shifted to the middle where he knew Bella could see him. "When we go in to be interviewed, I'll try and arrange it where we get you in and out as soon as possible. Act like you're a little offended at having to come in today. Not too much. We don't want you to become the focus of attention by having a snitty attitude.

"Snitty?" asked Heather. "Is that another of your made-up words?"

"Add it to your lexicon of southern words and phrases. It describes how you acted toward Captain Loving after you saw him kiss Alexandria yesterday."

"Thanks for reminding me."

Steve's mention of the kiss brought it afresh to Heather's memory. The man she'd been dating for months had not only been kissed by another woman, but he'd also done nothing to push her away. In fact, he'd been a willing participant. Had it been only twenty-four hours?

Heather used the travel time to examine her relationship with Charles Loving. She kept a full schedule, and not one that allowed much time for her love life. Ha, what love life? Their respective jobs had kept their times together infrequent. How often had they been out to eat? Did they ever see a movie together? She glanced at both hands and counted off the dates. She didn't need ten fingers. There had been no talk of a future together. Why did she feel betrayed?

She took the exit off the interstate. In mere minutes, she'd be face to face with Charles Loving.

# CHAPTER 20

Steve, Heather, and Bella stood outside the office of Captain Charles Loving. The door gaped open, and he waved the three of them in. Heather swallowed, held her head erect, and led the way. Glancing around, she found the office looked exactly like it did the last time she came to take Charles to lunch. Heather twitched a finger on her left hand. She'd forgotten to count that date. Two fingers remained to make the count an even ten. They'd been together eight times in three months. Most of the dates were lunches she had managed to shoehorn into her schedule.

Charles rose from his chair. "Thanks for coming. Have a seat."

Three chairs had been moved in front of his metal desk. The office reflected Captain Charles Loving perfectly. Things appeared straight, orderly, and efficient, with a hint of history. Two shadow boxes provided the only non-utilitarian touches to the décor. The first contained a display of various jail keys. The second, slightly larger in size, housed a collection of vintage handcuffs. Bookcases contained only books and binders related to law enforcement.

"Can I get any of you something to drink?" asked Captain Loving.

"None for me," said Steve.

Heather shook her head, as did Bella. "Are we to be interviewed in here?" asked Heather.

Charles took a seat. "Based on our conversation yesterday, I assumed you wanted to keep the interview formal. I've asked two of our detectives to speak to each of you separately. Any problem with that?"

Heather didn't like the separation but realized if she were in the shoes of the police, she'd prefer to divide witnesses to a crime and interview them individually. That way, they couldn't influence one another's memory of what happened.

"I told you yesterday I'll be acting as Bella and Steve's attorney. Due to the unique situation in our partnership, I'd like Steve to hear what Bella has to say."

Steve interrupted. "We intend to fully cooperate. We're aware this is not the way you prefer to conduct interviews, but because of our backgrounds, I think you'll find this will save time and facilitate a complete recounting of what happened." Steve smiled and waited for a response.

Captain Loving nodded his head. "No problem. What else?"

"I'd like you to question us," said Heather. "Some of the things we have to say, you'll wish you'd heard first hand. Also, you'll need to see our reactions in person and not rely on second-hand information or a grainy video."

Charles pushed his lips to one side and raised his eyebrows. "It might be crowded with six of us in a small interview room."

"Let one of the detectives observe through the glass," said Steve.

"Agreed." He pushed away from his desk. "Let's get started."

All four rose and made their way down a hallway. The interview room had a metal table bolted to the floor. A couple of large eye-bolts protruded through the table. Handcuffs could be looped through them for the more disagreeable interviewees. Except for a large mirror on one wall and a blinking camera stationed high in a corner, the room had the charm of a jail cell. Captain Loving brought a chair from his office and placed it beside two others. Heather settled Steve on one chair and sat Bella between them.

A second man came in and shut the door. Captain Loving introduced Detective David Schmidt. Schmidt reminded Heather of a block of granite. Head, chin, shoulders, and hips seemed square. A high and tight haircut accentuated the angles and telegraphed he'd been in one of the armed services, most likely a Marine. He possessed piercing gray eyes and the ability to hide emotion like a sphinx.

Captain Loving recited the preamble, giving the names of those present and the purpose of the interview.

Following this, Steve cut in. "Before we get started, we want to tell you again that we intend to fully cooperate with your questions to the best of our ability. We understand this is a serious matter, and we don't want to interfere with your murder investigation. However, we've been retained by Bella Brumley to find her birth parents. The course of our inquiry has already led us to contact several people that you may find of interest in your investigation. It's inevitable our paths will overlap. In fact, they already have."

The two policemen looked at each other. Captain Loving said, "We appreciate any information you might be able to give us. Who did you find of interest?"

"Why don't we take care of Bella first?" asked Steve. "We'll need to excuse her from some of the information we'd like to share with you."

Heather and Steve had coached Bella earlier that morning. They wanted to draw attention away from her, but to do that, Bella would need to do a little play-acting.

Bella stared at Heather like she'd been betrayed.

"Don't worry. Steve and I know what's best for you."

"That's what people have been telling me all my life." She folded her arms across her chest.

Heather patted Bella's arm and said, "Start yesterday morning when you first woke up and tell what you can remember in your own words."

Bella huffed at first but soon settled into a narrative that focused on the events leading to the shooting. Her attention to detail had both policemen nodding their heads. Twice they asked for additional information which she answered with ease.

The question Heather had been waiting for came from Detective Schmidt. "I checked your social media posts. You had some harsh things to say about your dad, including you'd like to shoot him. How do you explain that?"

"My adoptive dad," said Bella. "I wrote those things after I found out he'd signed a contract for me to wear next to nothing while they filmed me casting a fishing rod." She blushed and looked at her lap. "Things wiggle when I cast a rod. How would you like it if someone had control of your teenage daughter and put her in front of a camera practically naked?"

Heather interrupted. "After she leaves, we'll give the names of several people who can verify how Blake Brumley exploited Bella and how he intended to do even more in the future. As for the threats, they were nothing more than the ramblings of a teenage girl. Bella took no action to carry out the threats. She told us she didn't discuss harming Blake with anyone in person. As you well know, social media allows people to give voice to things they never do."

Bella's head nodded in agreement. "The only one I ever mentioned it to was Mike."

"Mike?" asked Detective Schmidt.

"My dog."

Steve held empty hands, palms up. "Feel free to question him. We can't get Mike to tell us anything."

The laughter had the intended effect of lightening the mood. Bella passed the test and had done an excellent job of portraying herself as the exploited, innocent girl she really was.

"I think we have what we need from Bella," said Captain Loving. "Why don't you go to my office and wait." He looked at her. "Can you find your way?"

Her chair scraped the vinyl floor as she stood and pushed her mane of hair over her shoulders. "If I didn't get lost tracking a wounded impala in the bush of Africa, I don't think I'll get lost in a narrow hallway in Conroe, Texas."

After the door closed, Captain Loving said, "That's quite a young lady."

Heather nodded. "She's special, all right." She straightened her back. "Let's continue, shall we?"

Steve took over. He started with Olin Field. "Bella calls him Uncle Olin. He was Blake Brumley's pilot until Blake fired him several months ago. Bella doesn't know why."

Detective Schmidt asked, "You haven't interviewed him?"

Heather said, "What we know about Mr. Fields comes through an internet search and second-hand sources."

Steve continued. "It's our understanding he contacted Jolene Cox and Gwen Fontaine, Bella's former teacher."

"I already know about Ms. Fontaine," said Detective Schmidt. "She called asking if we were assigning police protection to Bella."

"What did you tell her?" asked Steve.

"I told her Bella's living with two ex-cops. She reminded me of a helicopter parent hovering over their kid."

Heather changed the subject. "We searched for personal records on Bella. We were struck by what we didn't find. We couldn't locate adoption papers, shot records, or Bella's passport. Did your men find them? We left the safes open. All the safes, that is, that Bella knew about."

The two lawmen traded glances. Both shook their heads. Detective Schmidt broke the silence. "I was going to ask if you took those records. With the international travel she does, there must be a passport someplace in the house. I'll have another look."

Heather glanced toward the ceiling and noticed the red light blinking on the camera mounted high in a corner. It was easy to forget you were being recorded.

"Let's talk some more about Gwen Fontaine," said Captain Loving. "Anything unusual or suspicious about her?"

"She smells good and has a soft voice," said Steve. After the chuckles, Steve said, "The only thing remotely odd I could see was that she found out where Bella was staying because Olin Field called her."

Heather added, "Ms. Fontaine and Bella have a very close relationship. Blake Brumley fired Gwen when he thought she had something to do with a non-existent Romeo and Juliet relationship between Bella and D'Artagnan, AKA Dart, Salinsky."

Detective Schmidt let out a huff of disgust. "We know about Dart. I talked to him yesterday. He's got quite the attitude, not to mention a smart mouth."

"That's because you didn't talk dog with him," said Steve. "Heather and I got along fine with him, but only after we spoke his language. Did you tell him you owned a German shepherd?"

The detective's gaze fixed on Steve. "How did you know I own a shepherd?"

"I knew you owned a dog. My sense of smell is exceptional. I guessed on the breed. The cadence of your voice told me you were a Marine." He paused. "Sorry about the past tense. I know it's once a Marine, always a Marine."

The detective's posture stiffened. Steve continued. "As far as Dart is concerned, if you don't tell him you're the caregiver of a dog he shuts you out. Dart doesn't respond well to the idea of pet ownership. He puts animals on the same plane as humans. Some animals he ranks higher."

"What did you learn about Mr. Salinsky that we don't know?" asked Captain Loving.

"He claims to have never touched a gun. If he's telling the truth, I can't see him putting a .416 Remington Magnum to his shoulder and not coming away with a bruise on his cheek. Heather told me his face didn't have a mark on it. We didn't check his shoulder, but he washed a pug and gave her a full massage the whole time we talked to him. That gun will bruise an experienced hunter, let alone a skinny kid who doesn't know how to shoot."

"Good point," said the detective, even though he said it through gritted teeth. "Anything else?"

"He told us something Bella had already revealed. Blake Brumley shot him when he came to try to rescue Bella's dog."

"We know about that. Blake didn't really shoot Dart."

Heather leaned forward. "Would you like a plastic wad from a shotgun hitting you in the back from less than ten yards away?"

The question didn't warrant an answer. The detective moved on. "You said something a minute ago that indicated Bella and Dart weren't romantically involved. Is that true?"

Heather nodded. "It was wishful thinking on Bella's part. Dart can't stand her because she's a hunter. Like we said, he came to rescue a dog from a house full of killers."

"One more thing," said Steve. "Dart told us a TV film crew came to the store and interviewed him an hour or so before they happened to be driving by the front of the mall when Blake Brumley was shot."

Captain Loving's eyes opened wider. "Alexandria interviewed him?"

Steve and Heather both nodded. The revelation rocked Charles Loving. His eyes shifted left to right, looking for an explanation he wasn't going to find in the tiny interview room.

Steve added another layer to the questions Captain Loving must have been asking himself. "It's our understanding she and her cameraman are on their way here. The station's lawyer will be with them."

From the look Charles gave her and the tone of his next words, Heather concluded he'd gone on defense. "You two have been very busy. Are you sure you're not trying to solve this murder by yourselves?"

Heather returned his stare.

Steve said, "We're telling you what we discovered in the course of our investigation to find Bella's mother and father. The people who might be able to help us are intersecting with your murder investigation. I told you this would happen."

Steve slapped his forehead. "How could I forget? Bella's adoptive mom called her this morning. She's somewhere in Canada hunting something big and hairy."

"We know," said Detective Schmidt. "I'll detain her as soon as she clears customs."

Heather concluded by saying, "Bella told us Jolene might have misplaced a .416 Remington Magnum several years ago. She was sketchy on the details, but we thought you might like that information, too."

Detective Schmidt asked for more information on the possible loss of the rifle, which Steve gave him. Captain Loving excused himself and left the room. His furrowed brow gave a strong indication he had a lot on his mind.

The interview concluded. "Can you find your way to the captain's office?" asked Detective Schmidt."

"Thank you, I know where it is," said Heather.

Bella had been banished to the hall. Heather considered knocking but pulled her clenched fist away at the last moment. Her interrogation of Charles Loving on matters of the heart would have to wait for another time, another day.

"Well, it looks like we're dismissed. Let's go home," said Heather.

"That wasn't as bad as I thought it would be," said Bella. Steve's hand rested on her shoulder as they walked to the parking lot.

"Good job," said Steve. "You gave them enough so they'll leave us alone and we can concentrate on trying to find your parents."

"What about who murdered Blake?"

They reached the car. Steve felt for the handle of the rear door. "So far we've been a step ahead of the police, but they have a ton of resources. We'll leave the murder of Blake to them." He grinned. "Of course, we might happen to stumble upon something else in the course of looking for your parents."

Heather started the engine. "Are we ready to go home? I've had enough sensory input for one day."

"Let's run by Bella's house and take another crack at finding her missing documents." Steve leaned forward. "Is Bella listening to tunes again?"

"Yeah. Speak low."

"You and I are going to the pet store at first light. There's something we need to check."

# CHAPTER 21

After three hours of searching in vain, Heather pushed a lock of auburn hair from her face and said, "Steve, I've had it. Let's get out of here."

Bella busied herself by putting the stuffed mouse on its stand. She reset the cobra to its striking position and closed the glass door to the display. Her head jerked to see a man coming through the front door.

"Uncle Olin!" shouted Bella.

A barrel-chested man with a protruding midsection gave Bella a big, two-armed hug. He looked to be in his mid-to-late forties and stood a couple of inches shorter than Bella. A jagged scar cut across his face. Jeans, boots, and a fluffy down coat fit the vibe of the house and property.

Heather looked at Steve. His eyebrows had lifted ever so slightly.

"Are you okay, Sugar?" asked the man Bella had identified as her uncle.

Olin's thick brown hair became fully visible once he removed his tan cowboy hat. Heather noted a few stray strands of silver woven into the wavy mop that hung halfway down his ears. A rusty walrus-like mustache draped over his top lip.

"I'm okay, not great, but okay." Bella turned to look at Heather and Steve. "They were with me when it happened, and they're going to help me find my momma and dad."

The right eye of the man named Olin squinted as he took a long, suspicious look at Heather and Steve. His gaze shifted to Bella. "Why would you want to try and find the people who gave you up?" He paused and took a step away from her. "I'm sorry, Bella. This isn't the time or place to discuss that. I'm here to see what you need."

Steve took a step forward. "Before this gets too awkward, why don't we introduce ourselves? I'm Steve Smiley, and this is my business partner, Heather McBlythe."

Olin broke in. "What business are you in, Mr. Smiley?"

"Heather and I are private investigators."

"I'm also an attorney," said Heather. "Bella is my client." She issued a half-smile and continued. "Because a homicide has been committed, I have to be mindful of who Ms. Brumley speaks to and what she says. Can you tell me your full name and your relationship to Bella and Blake Brumley?" Heather believed a strong offense beat being on defense.

"My name is Olin Ray Field. Blake and I have been friends since grade school. I've known Bella since Blake brought her home. I thought I knew quite a bit about Blake and Bella. I didn't know he'd hired you to help her find her birth mother."

"Are you kidding, Uncle Olin?" asked Bella. "Blake didn't hire them. I did. They were right by us when Blake was shot."

Olin and Heather exchanged wary glances. He returned his gaze to Bella and took her by her hands. "Honey, you're a big girl, but I want you to think hard about what you're doing. Blake has lawyers you can use. I'm afraid you're going to get a big heartache when you look for the folks who gave you up." He leaned into Bella and whispered, "What do you know about these two?"

Steve's keen hearing paid off again. "Bella, what Olin says is good advice. You don't know either of us. We should go to a computer so you can do a check on us. Olin, I know you're wondering if we're after Bella's money. We're not. We don't need it."

Heather broke in. "My services to Bella are pro bono. We only take cases that interest us."

Steve added, "This one is unusual. We've never tried to solve a murder and find long-lost parents at the same time."

Olin stuck his thumbs in the front pockets of his jeans and leaned back. "Whoever her mother is, that woman walked away from Bella a long time ago. I doubt there's a father that even knows about her. I don't like the idea of you giving her false hope."

"We've already discussed this," said Steve. "She's well aware the chances are not good that we'll be able to do what she desires."

Olin again shifted his gaze to Bella. "I talked to your mom. She wanted me to ask if you want me to stay here with you."

Bella stiffened. "She's not my mom, and I won't be here."

Olin's eyes widened. "What do you mean you won't be here? Where will you be?"

"She's staying with me," said Heather.

Suspicion filled Olin's next questions. "With you? Where?"

"At my home in Spring. Here's my card. Call if you need to contact me. Or call Bella. I assume you and Jolene Cox have Bella's cell number?"

"I do. I'm not sure about Jolene."

"Bella's adoptive mother doesn't have her phone number?" asked Steve.

"I already told you," said Bella. "Blake bought out Jolene's share of me. We haven't spoken in years."

"I see," said Steve. "Will Ms. Cox be involved in the funeral arrangements?"

Olin shrugged that he didn't know.

"No, she won't," said Bella. "Why should she?"

Heather answered, "There's a great deal of money at stake. It's possible she could make a claim for being appointed your guardian."

Bella winced. "She's not going to worm her way in now."

"Hold on, Bella," said Olin as if he were reasoning with a petulant child. "She should be responsible for things like this now that Blake's gone."

Heather said, "Until official documents are found, we don't know if Bella is a minor or if she's reached her majority."

"Her what?" asked Olin.

"If she's an adult in the eyes of the law," said Steve.

The rubbing of his chin took a couple of seconds longer than it should if Olin had another objection. Was he stalling for time? Did he know about the driver's license?

Steve came to Olin's rescue. "Bella needs someone to help with the funeral. So far, it's only Heather and me. It doesn't sound like Jolene Cox is part of Bella's life any longer. With the victim being a television personality, I'm sure considerations need to be made for his fans." Steve paused. "Do you think Jolene will be back soon? Will she even come to the funeral?"

"I guess she will," said Olin, in a none-too-confident tone.

"Why? She hated Blake," said Bella.

The question went unanswered.

"Mr. Field, where were you yesterday at the time of the shooting?" asked Steve.

Olin rocked on his heels.

"The reason I'm asking is that the police will ask you the same thing. They already know you were Blake's pilot until he fired you. It's a standard question to rule out possible suspects. I purposefully sprung it on you to give you an idea of how serious this matter is. Go ahead, give me an answer, and I'll tell you if it sounds legitimate."

Olin shook his head. "You sound like a cop on TV. To answer your question, I was doing a walk-around on my airplane. I heard about the shooting on a TV they had playing in the hanger."

"Can anyone verify that?"

"Sure. There were pilots around. I can get you their names."

Steve issued a warm smile. "The police will need that, but we would like a copy of the list too. By the way, you did great and passed with flying colors. Do you see how intimidating police questioning can be?"

Olin ran a hand from his bushy mustache to his chin. "Man, you had me wondering if I needed a lawyer."

"By the way," said Steve. "Do you know Jolene Cox very well?"

"I used to. We haven't talked in quite a while. If we do talk, it's about Bella."

"Any idea where she might have been at the time of the shooting?"

Olin pressed his lips together and gave his head a nod. Realizing Steve couldn't see him, he said, "She called from Canada. I'm not sure exactly where."

"No problem. The police will find out."

"Why would they do that?"

"Ex-wives get special scrutiny."

Rays of the setting sun shone through the tops of the windows as shadows crept up the walls, giving the animal heads yet another burial of sorts. Heather shivered. "I don't know about the rest of you, but I'm ready to go home."

"Me, too," said Bella. "We didn't find anything."

"What are you looking for?" asked Olin.

"My stuff," said Bella. "My passport and other documents I'll need for travel."

Heather added, "It's important we learn as much as we can about Blake Brumley so I can give Bella sound legal advice."

Heather's answer was intentionally vague.

"Don't you have to have a search warrant or something?"

Heather considered the question and found it a little odd. Was he protecting Bella, or did something else cause his sudden interest in proper search procedures? She issued an emotionless answer. "The Sheriff's department searched yesterday. It's standard procedure for them to search the victim's residence after a homicide. Since they're finished, Bella can give us permission to look at anything in the home or on the property."

Olin's gaze went toward the windows facing the driveway and to Bella. "I guess if there's nothing I can do for you, I'll be going. I only came by to make sure you were all right."

Steve saved Olin from tripping over any more words. "Thanks so much for stopping by and checking on Bella. If you hear from Ms. Cox, tell her Bella is in good hands. She can call if she has any questions or concerns."

After a quick hug with Bella, Olin Field made for the door. He climbed into a relic of a Dodge pickup, gunned the engine and chugged away with a trail of blue smoke following him.

Steve asked, "Does Uncle Olin come here often?"

"He used to come almost every day. That was before Blake fired him."

"Did Olin teach you how to shoot?"

"He's better at tracking than shooting. He did help me calculate elevation and compensating for wind. He had a way of making me understand."

Heather took Bella by the sleeve of her camo shirt. "Let's make sure all the doors are locked and go get something to eat. What are you hungry for?"

"Pizza!"

# CHAPTER 22

Heather ran a brush through her hair, but only for a few strokes. A serious case of bedhead warranted drastic measures. Gathering the tangled mess, she pulled it into a ponytail and went looking for a baseball cap. Pre-dawn adventures with a blind man didn't warrant styled locks, let alone makeup.

She stepped into the coldest part of the day and raised her hand to knock on Steve's door. It swung open in front of her and out stepped Steve. Bathed, shaved and dressed for the day, he plowed past her with a spring in his step.

"I don't see why we couldn't have done this at a more reasonable hour," said Heather, trying to keep up with his pace.

Steve didn't reply. He had the route to Heather's car memorized so he didn't need her to guide him through shadows only she could see.

She shivered and started the car. Steve must have heard her teeth chattering. "Something tells me I shouldn't trust you climbing on top of a building until

135

you get caffeinated. Go to that diner on the way to the interstate. I didn't eat much supper last night. Pizza two nights in a row is too much for a guy my age."

"I thought you were in a hurry to get to the pet store?"

Steve folded his hands in his lap. "We have time."

Heather huffed out a cloud of condensation mixed with fatigue. "I don't know about you, but I need a break from a certain teenage girl. I'm not used to sharing my townhome with anyone, much less a late-night guest. Did you know Gwen came over last night?"

"I heard her voice through the pet door." Steve changed the subject and asked, "Are the seat heaters turned on?"

Heather reached and pushed two buttons. "Thanks, I'm not fully functioning yet." She returned to her previous thought. "Why didn't you come over?"

He kept his head facing forward but said, "Absence makes the heart grow fonder."

Neon signs blinked ahead. Heather wheeled into the diner's parking lot before the car had a chance to overcome the cold. No matter; a hot stimulant awaited them.

First light filtered through the east-facing window of the diner as Heather finished her third cup of coffee. She looked out on a sky with streaks of reds and purples. Her focus shifted to Steve as he nursed his second cup. "I'm awake enough to carry on a conversation. What's on your mind?"

"The pet store's security cameras. There has to be one covering the rear of the store. It should have captured the image of the person that climbed on the roof."

"If Dart's smiling face isn't on the store's surveillance tape, it explains why the police didn't arrest him."

Steve could turn things and look at multiple explanations. "What if the cameras weren't working? What if only the camera covering the back wasn't working?"

Heather grimaced as she drank the cold dregs. "I guess we'll know more after I climb a ladder."

"That may not be necessary. This isn't the movies where the police overlooked a key piece of evidence. I want you to check out the security camera. If you can stay on the ground and look through your fancy binoculars, that may be good enough. Look to see if a wire has been cut or disconnected."

"What if the camera and wires look good?"

"You may have to sweet-talk Captain Loving. I bet he'll let you peek at the crime scene investigation report."

Heather only had time to mumble a reply before the waitress slid an egg white omelet in front of her. She then delivered a breakfast fit for a lumberjack to Steve. Heather cut his slab of ham and a short stack of buttermilk pancakes. She drenched them in blueberry-maple syrup.

Steve demolished half his food before she asked, "What else did you have planned for us to do today?"

"We'll blast Bella out of bed and go to Conroe. I'm interested in knowing more about Olin Field. By the time we get there, his store will be open and any morning rush should be over."

"I'll need at least thirty minutes to tame the mane and change into something that doesn't make me look like a cat burglar."

"Take your time. After two days of running, we need a slower day."

# CHAPTER 23

Heather's hand reached to cover a yawn. "That was a wasted trip to the pet store. I can't believe you talked me into climbing on the luggage rack of my car to look at a security camera."

"I wanted to make sure," said Steve. "At least we know the wires weren't cut or disconnected." He leaned forward. "Aren't we there yet?"

Heather turned off the main road. Field's Electrical Supply Company sat in a tired cluster of businesses on a well-worn street. With all its repaired potholes, the street looked like it suffered from an industrial form of chickenpox. A few towering pine trees remained of what had once been a forest until progress visited Conroe, Texas. The tin-sided building looked functional but held no curb appeal.

"It's not as big as I was expecting," said Heather.

The front doorbell ding-donged as Steve, Heather, and Bella entered. Vintage country music streamed through speakers in the ceiling. A narrow-shouldered woman in her early fifties looked above the top of halflensed glasses and let out a squeal. "Bella? Is that you, honey?" She rounded a counter and gave a hug that would crush a lesser girl.

"Hi, Miss Emma," replied Bella. "Is Uncle Olin here?"

"Oh, honey, let me look at you." She held on to Bella's hands and took two steps back. "My goodness, you look prettier than you do on television." She came forward a step and spoke in a more discrete voice. "I'm so sorry to hear about Blake. Are you doin' all right?"

Bella nodded and took care of introductions with her right arm holding on to Miss Emma's slender waist. Olin Field did not make an appearance. Miss Emma, clad in jeans and a cable-knit sweater, continued to gush compliments and condolences. The woman had an exceptional gift for gab if such a thing could be called a gift.

Steve found a small opening and asked, "We came to visit with Olin. Is he here?"

"He took off a half-hour ago. No idea when he'll return." She looked at Bella. "He's taking Blake's death hard."

Steve nodded to indicate he understood. "Heather, why don't you leave Olin a note on his desk?" He faced Miss Emma. "Is that alright?"

Miss Emma waved off the question like it didn't matter who went into the office. "Fine and dandy." Her countenance clouded. "I'm worried about him. He opened this morning and stayed a spell, but then he headed for parts unknown with a big frown on his face."

"Bella, honey, take her on back to the office. There's a pen and paper on the desk. I'll make sure he sees it when he gets back."

"I'll stay here," said Steve.

Heather knew Steve well enough to realize he was up to something. She wasn't sure what, but he wouldn't be sending her into Olin Field's office unless he wanted her to look for something. While Bella jotted a quick message, Heather scanned the office. Framed photos and Olin's personal effects caught her eye. From what she saw in the photos, Olin Fields was passionate about flying, and Bella had captured his heart. Eight-by-tens covered a large portion of the office walls. They chronicled Bella's growth and rise to stardom as a hunter and television personality. Photos of Olin standing by a variety of airplanes took up a fair amount of wall space. Blake Brumley appeared in many of the pictures, but not as many as the attractive dark-haired woman they'd shared lunch with the previous day. Bella moved to Heather's side and sighed. "I miss Gwen. I hated Blake for firing her."

Heather studied a photo and said, "Gwen's very pretty and has kind eyes."

Miss Emma eased into the doorway and joined the conversation. "Gwen's been like a momma to Bella. I swear that woman is sweet as spun sugar."

Heather found a notepad on the cluttered desk and wrote a short note, then turned to Bella. "I think we better go. We still have some things to do today."

After a final hug, Bella extracted herself from Miss Emma's clutches and made for the parking lot. Steve and Heather delayed as Bella climbed into the car. Steve whispered, "What did you see?"

"Pictures. Lots of framed photos of Olin, Blake, Bella, and Gwen. They went to so many countries."

"Anything else?"

"Olin thinks the world of Bella, and Bella loves her teacher." Heather leaned in closer to him. "I also think Olin is carrying a torch for Gwen. He has seven framed photos of Bella and Gwen together."

"Anything else?"

"No."

"I didn't think so. Let's search the house again. You and Bella might have better luck today."

"Fine with me. I'm glad to get out of there. I don't think I can take another country song about cheating on your wife."

# CHAPTER 24

Heather pulled alongside the keypad of Big Blake's elaborate entrance only to see red and blue lights in her rearview mirror. A sheriff's deputy eased behind her car.

Heather rolled down her window as the officer approached.

"Ma'am, I'll need to see your driver's license and proof of insurance."

Heather gathered the documents from her purse and handed them over. Before the officer returned to the computer in his vehicle, he asked, "What's your business here?"

"I live here," said Bella.

"And I'm her attorney," said Heather as a post-script.

"Wait here. I'll be right back."

The officer retreated to his SUV and returned a short time later. "Detective Schmidt is on his way. He wants you to go in. He also said he's glad you came. The officers that were here misplaced the codes to the gate and the house."

Steve chuckled from the back seat. "It was probably the corporal that fainted after being attacked by a rubber snake."

Heather's driver's license and insurance card came through the window along with a chuckle. The officer bent over and took off a pair of wrap-around sunglasses. "Two and a half million YouTube views so far. The corporal decided to take off a couple weeks."

Heather drove down the tree-lined lane until she caught a glimpse of sunlight bouncing off the windshield of a truck parked in front of the house. She slowed to a crawl and looked to her right. "Do you know of anyone who should be here?"

Bella shook her head. Heather moved off the pavement and motioned the deputy to come forward. "Someone's parked in the driveway. Bella doesn't think they should be there."

The officer squinted to try to get a look at the vehicle in the distance. "I'll call for back up."

Two additional deputy patrol SUVs joined the first and moved toward the home. A fourth vehicle, an unmarked black Crown Vic sped past. "There's Detective Schmidt," said Heather.

"Let's join the party," said Steve.

As they approached, Bella said, "That's Uncle Olin's truck."

"Are you sure?" asked Steve.

"It's the same truck that was here yesterday," said Heather. "I couldn't make it out due to the distance and the trees blocking my view."

"Interesting," said Steve.

They mounted the steps and entered the great room. Mounts had been pulled off the wall. A desk lay with its legs facing the ceiling, and a knife had ripped into the hide of a zebra skin covered chair. Olin Field stood with his hands fastened behind him with chrome-plated handcuffs.

Bella rushed toward him, but an officer blocked her path. Heather moved to her side and made sure she didn't interfere.

Detective Schmidt cast a suspicious glance at Heather, Steve, and Bella. "For a house that's supposed to be empty, we have quite a few people here."

"We came to get more clothes for Bella," said Steve to counter the detective's suspicions. "Your boys weren't too keen on letting us leave with much for Bella to wear."

Heather pointed to Bella. "Look at her. She had to wear my clothes today." She didn't tell him Bella was thrilled to put on something besides camo.

Bella's eyes filled with tears. "Why, Uncle Olin? What were you looking for?"

Regret and remorse lined his face. "I'm sorry to tell you this, but Blake owed me a lot of money. I purchased a new twin-engine airplane, then he fired me and left me holding the bag. I still can't believe he did that after all

145

I've done for him. I'm drowning in debt. I thought if I could find the gold he stashed here in the house, I could make the payments on the plane until I can sell it."

Detective Schmidt kept his eyes on Olin but spoke to one of the deputies. "Be sure to read him his rights and put him in an interview room. I'll be along to question him and file charges."

The deputy took Olin by the arm and took a step toward the door. Bella began to plead for Olin. "Can't you let him go? I don't want to press charges. It doesn't matter to me if he cut that stupid chair." Her hand swept the room. "It's Blake's fault. He made Uncle Olin buy the plane and then he fired him. Blake owed him the money. As soon as I can, I'll give it to him."

Heather turned to face Bella and put her hands on the teen's shoulders. "It doesn't work that way in this state. Burglary of a habitation is a felony. When Olin destroyed property, it added at least one additional charge. The police have no option but to arrest him." She took Bella by the hand. "Don't worry, I'll get him out of jail after he appears before a judge and bond is set."

"That won't be until tomorrow morning," said Detective Schmidt.

Steve asked Heather to lead him to a chair. He settled himself and directed his words to Detective Schmidt. "Since we're here and you're down a deputy, how would you like Heather and Bella to help you look for the missing documents? If Olin was telling the truth, there's a pile of gold, too."

The detective hesitated. Bella nodded with enthusiasm and tacked on a syrupy, "Please."

Detective Schmidt shrugged. "Why not? Bella can help me search. Heather can help one of the deputies."

Steve asked, "You didn't happen to bring a metal detector, did you? It might come in handy."

"Good idea," said the detective. "I'll call for one."

Hours clicked by as the search of the home progressed with no results. The sun slipped behind the pines about the same time a deputy brought the metal detector upstairs to Blake's bedroom. Heather pushed a lock of hair behind her ear and huffed as she and a deputy pulled Blake's king-size bed away from the wall. She guessed the log bed weighed several hundred pounds. On hands and knees, Heather examined the wall behind the bed for anything unusual. She observed nothing but pristinely painted sheetrock.

"This metal detector is pretty useless inside," said the deputy. "I'm getting hits on drywall screws and echoes from nails when I scan the floors."

Heather moved to the foot of the bed. "Let's push this beast back in place." The deputy tapped his class ring on the vertical post of the footboard. "I thought I wanted a log bed. If they're this heavy, I'll stick with what I have."

Heather looked at the deputy. "Tap that log again."

He did and moved to the other vertical post. His ring struck it three times. He looked at her with eyes wide. The first gave off a hollow pitch. The second

147

sounded a higher note. He spoke to the deputy that brought the metal detector. "Scan these posts."

The metal detector didn't react to the second post the deputy's ring had struck. The first, however, sent the machine screeching. It didn't take long before the deputies found a seam, popped the top off the post and retrieved three long sleeves of gold coins. A check of the top two posts of the headboard revealed a treasure trove of gold bars and coins stashed inside the hollowed out sections of eastern red cedar.

Detective Schmidt came upstairs and shook his head at the sight of gold coins and bars spilled across the bedspread. Bella squealed when she caught sight of the glimmering treasure.

The sound of footsteps and the tapping of the tip of a cane preceded Steve standing in the doorway. "Did someone strike gold?"

"The motherlode," said Heather.

Bella pinched her eyebrows together. "Why did Blake have so much gold?"

Nobody gave an answer. Heather looked at Steve. Instead of providing some sort of response to Bella's question, he asked, "Still no luck in finding the paperwork on Bella?"

"Not yet," said Detective Schmidt."

Steve rubbed his chin. "Did you look in the return air vents?"

Bella said, "Yeah, we found three on the bottom floor, one in the basement and two on the second floor."

"There's three on the first floor?" asked Detective Schmidt. "I thought there were only two."

Bella shook her head. "I pulled the covers off three, including the one in Blake's office. The love seat sits in front of it. I looked at it when you went to the bathroom. I had the cover back on, and the love seat moved back by the time you returned. I took them off just like you told me to, but I didn't see anything.

"What do you mean you didn't see anything?" asked Steve. "Did they have filters in them?"

"Yes."

"Did you pull out the filter to see what was behind it?"

"I didn't know the filters came out."

Steve stepped out of the way as Detective Schmidt hurried past him. He shouted over his shoulder to his deputies. "Wrap that gold in the bedspread and bring it downstairs. No souvenirs!"

Heather, Steve, Bella, and one of the deputies followed. It didn't take long before metal grates lay on the floor of the great room along with their filters. Other than needing replacement, nothing of note existed behind them. Blake's office held the final return air vent.

Heather turned to Bella. "Who does the housecleaning?"

"Gwen did it until Blake fired her. After that, he hired a service. They weren't near as thorough as Gwen."

Detective Schmidt removed the metal cover and pulled out the filter. "At last," he said with a smile parting his lips. He removed a ten-inch by twelve-inch gray fire safe by its black handle and turned to Bella. "Any idea where the key to this is?"

Her head shook from side to side. "I've never seen it before, let alone the keys."

Steve covered a yawn. "If it's all right with you detective, we'll get some clothes for Bella and get out of here. Heather can stop by tomorrow and take a peek at what's in the safe."

"I'll check with Captain Loving on that. If nothing else, I'll have a list of the contents typed for her."

Heather cast her gaze at Bella. "Why don't you and one of these deputies go to your room and get whatever clothes you think you might need? Steve and I will be in the car."

After bidding Detective Schmidt and the deputies good night, Heather led Steve outside. She closed the front door with more firmness than necessary. "Why are we running away? Don't you want to know what's in the safe or how much gold there is?"

Steve stopped on the front porch. "Sure I do, but if there are documents relating to Bella's adoption in that safe I don't want her to know about it until we've had a chance to examine them."

Heather thought for a moment. "Do you think Bella's adoption might not have been kosher?"

Steve rested his hands on the top of his cane. "Does Blake Brumley impress you as a paragon of virtue?" He didn't wait for a response to the rhetorical question.

"You'll know soon enough. Tomorrow you'll examine what's in the safe. The adoption papers are the treasure we're looking for."

"What if they aren't in the safe?"

"We have two choices. We can keep looking or give up."

Heather led Steve down the front steps. "I know another reason you didn't want me to look in the safe tonight."

"Why?"

"Actually there are two reasons: First, you're hungry. If you don't get something in that growling stomach, you're going to be hard to live with."

"Guilty on the first count," said Steve. "And the second reason?"

"You don't want Bella keeping us from a good night's sleep by asking questions about how we're going to find her parents."

"You're half right," said Steve. "I don't want *you* losing another night's sleep. Bella's yours after supper." He paused. "One more thing. No pizza tonight."

# CHAPTER 25

Heather watched as Steve tucked a napkin into the front of what she knew to be his best shirt. He perched on a stool at the bar dividing his kitchen and dining room. With one finger inside the bowl, Steve poured milk onto his Frosted Shredded Wheat. When the two percent touched his fingertip, he stopped pouring. She said, "Don't you look dapper today."

He took a bite of cereal to avoid replying.

She retrieved a porcelain cup. It made a slight clink as it touched the marble countertop. The aroma of Sumatra dark roast blended with Steve's aftershave as he munched his cereal. Steve rarely splashed on aftershave.

"What are we going to do with Bella today?" Heather asked to get a conversation going.

"Bella's a big girl; we can leave her here," said Steve.

Several seconds passed as he lifted another bite. "We have a lot to do today," said Heather. "I need to drop you off at the office, take care of getting Olin Field out of jail, and find out what documents Detective Schmidt found."

"You forgot something," said Steve. "You have unfinished business with Captain Loving."

Heather released something between a sigh and a moan.

Steve raised his head. "If you'd rather I call him, I will. I'm curious to know what he found out about the coincidence of Alexandria Ramos being at the pet store and in front of the mall when Blake Brumley was killed."

Steve took another bite of cereal. Heather remained quiet, something she normally didn't do when planning out her day. After swallowing, he said, "You might as well get it over with."

"Get what over with?"

Steve dropped his spoon in the bowl and huffed a sigh of exasperation. "You're driving yourself crazy, wondering why Charles Loving and Alexandria Ramos were kissing. Ask him. You'll know where you stand."

Heather blew on the coffee to cool it. She also did it to stall for time while she pondered his straight-forward approach.

"You're right," she said with a firm nod of her head. "We need to know if she had advance warning about the shooting, and I need to know if I should sharpen my hook for another fish."

Steve released a soft chuckle. "Don't throw him back before you know what's going on."

The sound of coffee being poured into the sink must have reached his ears. He lifted his chin. "I take it you've made a decision."

"Let's go," said Heather with determination.

Steve balked. "I'm staying here to work on Blake's funeral arrangements."

"I thought you wanted me to help with that."

"You have things to do that I can't help you with. I'd only slow you down."

Heather considered his decision to stay home. The answer hit her. "You don't want to leave because Gwen is coming over. That explains the aftershave and wearing your nicest shirt."

Steve finished the last bite of cereal, rinsed his bowl, and placed it in the dishwasher. He turned to Heather. "Gwen called this morning and offered to help. She and Bella know the people to invite. I thought the funeral service would be held at Blake's house, but Gwen said the producers of Blake and Bella's show contacted her. They asked for her help and said she needed to make arrangements for a bigger venue."

Heather grinned at Steve's determination to minimize his desire to be around Gwen.

Steve rambled on. "It's time for us to maximize our resources. You have a list of things you need to do, and you don't need my help with any of them. Bella's adoptive mom, Jolene, is somewhere in Canada and apparently doesn't give a rip. Olin Field needs you to get him out of jail. For someone who is recognized by hundreds of thousands of people, Bella has only a few people that really know her. Gwen is the logical choice to orchestrate what promises to be an elaborate production."

"Does your decision to stay have anything to do with the fact that Gwen Fontaine is a very attractive woman with a voice that drips honey?"

"You forgot to add how good she smells," said Steve.

Heather sniffed the air around him. "She's not the only one."

Before she left, Heather made sure Steve settled himself in his recliner, even though he needed no assistance. Her gaze fixed on him. Why had he put on his best shirt this morning? Why did he take extra time showering and shaving? He even splashed on some of what he said Maggie had called smell-good stuff.

A knock preceded Steve issuing a command to enter. Heather gazed into Gwen's doe-like eyes. Her perfume floated into the townhome. "I'm leaving; he's all yours."

She winced when she realized what she'd said.

# CHAPTER 26

Olin Field's bond hearing went without a hitch. Due to him being a local business owner with no criminal record and a good reputation in the community, Heather suggested he be released on personal recognizance. An overworked Assistant District Attorney went for ten thousand dollars bond due to multiple charges. He also believed the zebra skin chair to be valuable, even though he couldn't say how much it might be worth. Heather contended Olin had codes to the house and the front gate and noted that Bella had stated she didn't care about the chair or any damages. The judge split the difference and set bond at five thousand dollars.

Olin made arrangements to pay five hundred dollars and promised to appear when called.

The hallway of the municipal building echoed with voices, but not enough so Heather couldn't talk to Olin. "Sorry, I thought I could get you out on a PR bond," said Heather. "I think the zebra-skin chair threw the judge for a loop. He had no idea how to value it."

Olin rolled his shoulders. "It's my fault for being stupid. I had no business going there without Bella." His eyebrows pinched together. "The cop that took me to jail said they were going to search the house again. Did they find anything?"

Heather shifted her briefcase into her other hand. "They found the gold you were looking for."

Before she could tell him where they'd found it, he asked, "Did they find anything else?"

"There was a small safe hidden in an air conditioner duct. I'm on my way to the Sheriff's office to find out what it contained."

"They wouldn't let you see last night?"

She shook her head and noticed how intense his gaze bore into her. She dismissed it due to the strain of being arrested, a sleepless night in jail, and an appearance in court.

"How is Bella?" he asked.

"She's more worried about you than anything else."

His shoulders slumped. "Bella's such a sweetheart. I'd do anything for that girl. What's she doing today?"

"She's with Steve and Gwen working on funeral arrangements."

A crowd of people spilled out of a courtroom and chatted their way toward them with no attempt at being quiet. Heather held out a hand in the direction of an exit. She spoke as they walked. "I hate to abandon you, but you'll need to find another attorney to take over. Bella's my client, and you broke into her house. I represented you at the bond hearing as a favor to her."

Olin nodded. "I understand. Thanks so much for what you did today, and what you're doing for Bella."

They reached a door, and Olin opened it for her. "By the way," said Heather. "Do you still have the airplane Blake wanted you to buy?"

He nodded. "I'm trying to hold on to it by doing charters. Emma and her husband can run the business whenever I'm gone. If you ever need to go somewhere, let me know."

Heather liked the idea of having a plane to fly her to places where she could see various investment possibilities and be home the same day. Her thoughts shifted to Captain Loving, and she said, "I need to go. Call Bella and tell her you're out of jail so she'll stop sending me texts."

Heather made her way to her vehicle, dreading the next stop she needed to make. Dreary overcast clouds carrying misty rain streamed from the Gulf of Mexico to push against the cold front that had blown through four days earlier. Heather turned off the intermittent wipers and parked in a narrow space at the Sheriff's office.

She'd compiled a list of things she needed to ask and hoped Detective Schmidt and Charles Loving would be forthcoming with the information they'd gathered. Those thoughts took a back seat to what had caused a restless night. Had she been replaced by a pretty television reporter? Like a corkscrew, that question burrowed into her mind and held fast. She gathered herself and strode into her uncertain future.

Charles must have heard her footsteps as he was already standing behind his desk when she entered. Detective Schmidt also rose and greeted her with a half-smile. A quick glance at Charles' desk revealed stacks of papers and documents. At first glance, she believed them to be the contents of the safe obtained the previous night.

Charles' outstretched hand bid Heather to have a seat. "Did you get Olin Field out on bond?"

She nodded. "Five grand and I told him to find another attorney."

"Did he stick with his story about looking for gold?" asked Detective Schmidt.

Again, she nodded her response.

Charles waved a hand over the pile of papers on his desk. "Here's what was in the safe. I knew you'd want to see for yourself."

"Do you want me to put on gloves before I examine them?"

Captain Loving grimaced and gave Detective Schmidt a withering stare. "If it were the gold, it wouldn't matter."

It only took her a moment to understand. "Someone compromised the evidence, didn't they?"

He nodded his answer and motioned with a slight jerk of his head to Detective Schmidt. "Tell her."

"The officer with the metal detector played like he was a pirate. He picked up handfuls and let them fall. His fingerprints are on multiple pieces."

The detective looked as if he wanted to crawl under a desk. He made for the relative safety of the hallway.

Captain Loving stood and walked around his desk. "Why don't you sit in my chair? You'll be more comfortable."

Heather noticed his excessive cordiality. "Is this everything?"

He nodded. "We videotaped opening the safe and cataloging the contents. If you want to see it, I'll be glad to show it to you." His gaze caught hers but only for a second before he looked away. "Take your time. Let me know if you need copies of anything."

"Before you go." She paused. "You forgot something."

His words came out staggered. "Well, yes. About that—"

Before he could stumble over any more sentences, she said, "Gloves, Charles. I need gloves."

Crimson rose into his face. "Top drawer on the left." His hand fumbled for the door handle as he looked over his shoulder. "I'll check to see how you're doing in ten or fifteen minutes."

A random memory flashed in Heather's mind. Her freshman year at Princeton she'd not prepared for a history exam that was to include several battles in the Napoleonic Wars. She'd been encouraged by her

160

roommate to write a few of the dates on a piece of paper, slip it under her watchband and wear a long sleeve shirt. If her memory failed, she'd pull up her sleeve and expose the note. Guilt overwhelmed her, and she discarded the cheat-sheet before she went into class. Had she looked as guilty as Charles did?

Putting the thought aside, she sat in the still-warm chair and began to review the documents. Bella's passport topped the heap. Stamps from immigration and customs officials dotted the pages until it was difficult to find an open spot. The passport was legitimate.

The bulk of the pile consisted of education progress reports written in the neat handwriting of Gwen Fontaine. A well-known home school curriculum had been chosen, and rigorously followed. Gwen had been a diligent teacher. Otherwise, there were immunization records in a file that included other medical-related documents. A social security card came out of a plain envelope. Again, this looked legitimate, but she made a note to verify. Fraud abounded with older Social Security numbers.

Heather leaned back in the chair and considered what she'd seen. A second check of the date of birth on the passport didn't match the driver's license Bella had given her. The day and month were the same, but the year didn't coincide. That didn't surprise her as Bella had stated Blake had given her a forged operator's permit.

After a light knock and a three-second wait, the door swept open, and Charles came in. He closed it and moved toward the chair in front of the desk. As Heather stood to surrender her seat to its rightful owner, he raised his hand for her to stop. "Please stay where you are. I'll sit on this side for a change." He asked, "Did you find anything helpful?"

Heather folded her hands in front of her as if she were going to pray. She leaned forward. "Except for the home school records and the social security card, these look like documents Blake would need to grab and go for international travel. No wonder he kept them in his office." Heather shook her head from side to side. "What's missing is a birth certificate or any court documents related to Bella's adoption. Those are the foundations on which Blake built her identification. They have to be somewhere. Where could Blake have put them? How did we miss them?"

Charles rubbed the lip that used to be the home of his handlebar mustache. He'd shaved it off because Heather didn't like it. "We're checking his financial dealings. We might find he had a safety deposit box. We're also going to sweep the yard and the shooting range with the metal detector."

"Good luck on the range," said Heather. "Between the lead and steel shot, that detector will go off before you get it out of the car."

A bead of perspiration formed on Charles' top lip. Heather found herself staring at the mound of documents. After several seconds Charles broke the silence. "We need to talk."

Heather didn't mean to, but she pounced on his words. "You're darn right we do. What's the story with you and that TV reporter?"

She regretted the tone and the pun but not the question. She'd been rightly accused of being too direct with her speech on several occasions.

Charles stopped rubbing his palms on his pants and fixed his gaze on her. "Her name is Alexandria Ramos. We were supposed to be married in a couple of weeks. She broke it off last spring when she took the job as a reporter."

What tasted like dirty chalk filled Heather's mouth. Her stomach dropped to someplace far below where the Lord intended it to be. She gathered herself and said, "And?"

Charles's head wagged from side to side. "I don't know."

A flash of Boston anger came upon her along with a bit of attorney training thrown in for good measure. "Explain your answer. What are your intentions? Do I need to buy a dress for the Christmas party you invited me to, or should I be looking for a wedding present? Will you need a toaster or a place setting of china for the future Mrs. Charles Loving? I'd like to know if it's not too much to ask."

Charles placed both hands on his face, pulled them down, and heaved a sigh. "I didn't intend to do anything to hurt you."

Heather stood. "What stores are carrying your selections? I'm sure Steve will want to give you something, too."

She leaned forward, her palms flat on his desk. Charles stammered something that she didn't catch. "What did you say?"

He squared his shoulders. "I said, I'm sorry. Alexandria is quitting her job." He paused. "That's not exactly true. She went off on her boss. He fired her."

If regret had a face, Charles Loving wore it. Heather plopped in her chair and sat in silence for twenty long seconds. Like the slow leak of air out of a balloon, her anger gradually released.

Charles must have sensed she'd calmed. A coy smile pulled the corners of his mouth. "Remind me to never get on the witness stand with you asking questions."

"Sorry, I didn't mean to grill you." Her cheeks puffed out, and she exhaled residual anger. "Would it be out of line if I asked you to tell me how Alexandria came to be at the pet store and the mall?"

The haze of mistrust and betrayal lifted. Despite the stings of rejection, Heather felt a rush of relief. They had returned to the firmer ground of professional conversation, away from the quicksand of bruised egos and battered feelings.

Charles sat erect but relaxed. "Alexandria received an anonymous call on Black Friday. A man told her to be at the north entrance of The Woodlands Mall at noon on

Saturday. He said it would make her career. She'd already been assigned to do a piece on pets as gifts for Christmas and used that as an excuse to travel to The Woodlands."

"Did Alexandria record the phone conversation?"

He nodded. "That's how I know it's a man that called. Unfortunately, he used a device to alter his voice."

Heather narrowed her gaze. "This sounds professional."

Charles nodded. "Alexandria gave me the recording. That's part of the reason she's not working there. The station's attorney blew a gasket when she found out Alex had given it to me and that she'd told me what she knew before she talked to her. Alex didn't make a copy for the station. Her boss went into a tirade about not revealing things related to confidential informants and protecting sources. Things got ugly. I'm still not sure if she quit or they fired her."

Heather cocked her head. "What aren't you telling me?"

He erupted in a laugh that distilled into a disarming smile. "You can be a very intimidating woman."

"What else? I can tell there's still something on your mind."

His head tilted to one side. "All right, counselor, I'll give you a full confession. I realized our relationship wouldn't last. I came to that conclusion before Alexandria and I saw each other again."

Heather bristled. "When were you planning on telling me about her?"

"I tried to tell you three weeks ago. You've been so busy working on that condo deal you didn't have time." His eyebrows lifted as he asked, "Do you know how many times you turned me down for lunch or supper in the last six weeks?"

Heather slowly shook her head. "I didn't keep count."

"Thirteen."

"Oh. I had no idea." Her stomach did another slow roll.

Before she could respond further, he moved on. "The rest of the story is Alexandria and I have been talking for the last month. For the first two weeks, it was nothing but phone conversations. Her job wasn't the glamour she thought it would be. After getting jilted last spring, I was afraid to move too fast."

"So you kept me on the bench in case the first-stringer didn't pan out?"

"See what I mean? You nailed me to the wall with a sports metaphor. How many women can do that? You're beautiful, polished, poised, incredibly smart, and driven to succeed more than any woman I've ever met. To give you a sports metaphor of my own, you're a major league star. I'm playing minor-league ball."

Heather stood, as did Charles. "I'm happy for both of you. I'm not saying that to be polite. She's a beautiful woman, and I wish you both the best."

166

"Thanks. Are you and Steve making progress in finding Bella's parents?"

"We're trying, but things aren't coming together yet. Steve, Bella, and Gwen Fontaine are at his townhome making arrangements for the funeral. I'll spend the rest of the day trying to find out more about Bella, but it's going to be hard without adoption papers. We're hoping when Jolene Cox gets back from Canada, she can shed some light on things."

"If her attorney allows her to talk. Detective Schmidt is convinced she killed Blake Brumley."

"Does he have proof?"

"There's the rifle. It's registered to Jolene Cox-Brumley. We also checked her social media. Bella's adoptive mother had some nasty things to say about Big Blake when they split. So far, we know she checked into the airport forty-eight minutes after the shooting. We timed it. She had time to take the shot and make it to the airport."

"You mentioned social media. Anything specific or recent?"

"Nothing recent but during and immediately after the divorce, she claims Blake hid two million dollars from the court."

Heather nodded. "How much gold did you find squired away in the log bed?"

"Take a guess," said Charles.

"Two million?"

Charles responded with a silent nod.

167

Heather glanced toward the door. "It will be interesting to see how she reacts to that little bit of news." She came around the desk, took a step toward the door, and stopped. "Do you think it might be possible for Steve and me to watch the interview from behind the glass?"

"I'll give you a call when we pick her up."

# CHAPTER 27

The roller tip of Steve's collapsible cane sounded like a single-wheeled in-line skate when he swept it in front of him. "You can't sneak up on anyone if you're using that cane," said Heather.

"There aren't many places dark enough for people not to notice me. Besides, this cane isn't like my other one. It folds into small sections, and I don't have to worry about people tripping over it."

They continued across the parking lot. In a complete non sequitur, Heather asked, "How long has it been since Blake was killed?"

"Today is day nine. Have you lost track of time?"

Heather stifled a yawn. "The first three days were a whirlwind. Without a birth certificate or adoption papers, I've hit a dead end. The only thing I've accomplished is learning more about missing children than I ever wanted to know. I've read until my eyes crossed and I've spoken to so many authors and experts I can't keep track of them. Even though I was in law enforcement, I had no idea of the scope of the problem."

"Hopefully, your research will pay off once we find the missing documents."

"I'm beginning to lose hope." Heather changed the tone of her voice. "Three more steps and I'll open the door."

Heather raised her eyebrows when Steve suggested they sit on a back row at the funeral. "Don't you want to be with Bella and Gwen?"

"I need you to whisper to me what you see. Gwen seemed wound tight this morning. I decided to give her some space."

Heather scanned the room as the line of people filed in. "The chapel can seat at least six hundred. I'm glad we're early. The way it's filling, there'll be standing room only in a few minutes."

Steve folded his cane into one-foot sections and felt his way into his seat. "Gwen gave an open invitation to the people on Blake and Bella's email list. The producers of his show wanted to make sure the room would be packed. That's why they waited more than a week after his death to have the memorial service. People in the film and hunting industries had to adjust their schedules. Not an easy task in the middle of deer season."

It didn't surprise Heather to see the event would be filmed, but she counted seven cameras on tripods. "What's the story on the film crews? I didn't expect so many."

Before Steve could answer, a request came from one of the funeral directors for people to move to the center of their aisle and make room for as many people as possible.

After resettling, Steve said, "I've been learning about show biz this week. Bella's producer and director wanted to make sure Blake's name didn't fade before they could transition the show to Bella. They arranged for local stations to be here. That doesn't include their film crews of the various television personalities. They made deals with several men like Blake to give eulogies."

"What do you mean, men like Blake?"

"Guys with their own hunting shows. Gwen's been fielding Bella's calls and taking care of logistics. She directed some to the producer and director if she couldn't answer their questions. For the most part, she's responsible for the service."

A polished wood casket stood in front of the stage. Heather asked, "I thought you said Blake was cremated?"

"The casket is for show. Blake's remains are in an urn at my place. The producer didn't want to offend Blake and Bella's fans who don't like the idea of cremation."

Heather's mind wandered from the scene in front of her. She'd been running into one roadblock after another in her quest to discover Bella's origins. Gwen had become Steve's confidant and a daily fixture at his townhome. She'd heard Christmas carols filter through the pet door. What other changes might be in Steve's future? And what changes might be in her future?

171

Instrumental gospel hymns faded as a side door opened at the front of the room. A grey-haired, somber-faced man wearing a black suit and a name tag led the way. When he reached the front row, he turned and extended a hand to direct Gwen, Bella, and Olin Field to their seats. Bella sat between the two adults. Her waist-length hair shimmered against a black long-sleeve dress that stopped a good four inches above her knees.

Heather squinted and shook her head. The dress wasn't completely black; it had a faint dark-green camo pattern woven in. Bella held a tissue and dabbed her eyes. Heather wondered if she'd been coached to cry.

"Gwen's on the left, Olin on her right and Bella's sandwiched between them. They look like a Hollywood family," said Heather.

Steve nodded but didn't respond. Had she said the wrong thing? Was that a scratch of jealousy in her voice? Gwen's increasing influence on Steve troubled her. A thought jumped into her mind. She'd already lost the company of Charles Loving. Would her relationship with Steve also be reduced to business only? Even though their relationship couldn't be more platonic, they'd settled into a routine of mutual trust and dependence.

Implacable Steve rarely revealed what went on in his keen mind. Her staring at him would gain no added insights, so she turned away and withdrew into her thoughts.

A tall man with a close-cropped gray beard stood behind a single microphone and began the service with the appropriate words. His rich voice caressed the crowd with an opening prayer, and he called the first man to offer a eulogy to come forward. The man stood but not before Dart Salinsky rushed to the microphone.

"Murderers! Killers! Why are you celebrating a man dedicated to taking so many lives? Stop the killing!"

Three men rushed to the podium. Cameras rolled. Two women and three men scattered in the crowd chanted, "Stop the killing! Stop the killing!"

A balled fist caught one of the male protesters square on the nose. Blood gushed. The crowd didn't wait for the police to clear the protesters. Incensed by the shouting, burly men and stout women sprang to action, forcing the protesters from the building.

Two local TV cameramen grabbed their cameras and followed the protesters out of the chapel with reporters talking over their shoulders into camera lenses.

Heather kept her mouth close to Steve's ear and gave him a running account of the melee. His head wagged side to side in disgust, but he made no attempt to speak above the shouts and screams.

Order eventually returned, and the service progressed with glowing eulogies and expressions of how unfair it was that the world lost such a wonderful man. Each speaker veered from their written remarks to speak candidly of the challenges they faced with what they termed, "Radicals intent on stripping hunters of their rights." After fifty minutes, the final "Amen" came from the officiant and people filed out. Steve continued to sit, so Heather made no move.

"How were the cameras arranged?" asked Steve.

Heather hadn't expected the question but remembered their placement. "One filmed Bella the entire time. Another scanned the crowd, looking for reactions. The third and fourth cameras filmed the speakers."

"Did you recognize anyone you didn't expect to be here?"

Heather chuckled and said, "None besides Dart Salinsky and his merry band of protesters."

A deep voice came from over her shoulder. "The show's over. Are you two going to spend the night here?"

Steve answered, "Captain Loving, I thought you'd be lurking in the shadows."

Steve and Heather both stood and moved out of the pew. Steve asked, "Is Detective Schmidt with you?"

"He's at the courthouse requesting a pocket warrant for Jolene Cox. She's scheduled to come back to Houston the day after tomorrow."

Heather came on point. "A pocket warrant? I can think of three reasons for wanting that. First, you want to give her a chance to explain the evidence against her before you serve the arrest warrant. Second, you don't want word to leak out that a judge has signed a warrant. Third, Detective Schmidt wants full credit for the collar. That warrant ensures it won't be put in the database. Only he will have it in his pocket." She smiled. "Which is it, Charles?"

"All three."

Heather shifted her gaze from Loving. Alexandria Ramos, some distance away, waited with her head lowered. She excused herself from the men and made for the woman who had won Charles Loving's heart. An extended hand acted as Heather's olive branch. Alexandria gave it a tentative shake and tried to release it. Heather squeezed it and moved closer. "You're a lucky woman. Charles is one of the finest men I know. I wish you much happiness." She loosened her grip. "Because of our jobs, he and I will cross paths from time to time. I want you to know whatever there was between us is over for good. I hope you and I will be friends."

Alexandria looked at her with wide brown eyes. Relief pried apart her lips. "I'd like that."

"Come on," said Heather with a tilt of her head. "Let's join the boys before they get into trouble."

Alexandria nestled herself under Charles' arm while Steve nodded a greeting. "Charles was telling me congratulations are in order. Have you set a date?"

Charles opened his mouth to speak, but Alexandria beat him to it. She spoke in a conspiratorial tone. "We're keeping the original date. It will be a small secret ceremony on the eighteenth. In the spring we'll have the big church wedding my momma has her heart set on. We're not going to tell our parents or hardly anyone else about the first wedding."

Steve lowered his voice and joined in the conspiracy. "Maggie and I did the same thing. Maggie's mom insisted her little girl be a June bride." He smiled. "We had other plans. The second semester of our senior year involved a minister sworn to secrecy, two witnesses and months of clandestine rendezvous in cheap motels. It felt like we were being naughty, but amazingly, it helped ease us into marriage. We learned to trust each other with a big secret, and we couldn't smother each other because we had part-time jobs and classes to finish."

Heather shook her head. She thought she knew Steve's secrets, but he'd come up with something that left her mouth agape.

Charles hugged his bride-to-be to his side. "It's a win-win. We'll be happy and so will the parents." His smile faded. "But now it's time we got back to work. We'll meet you there."

"Where are we going?" asked Heather.

Steve unfurled his cane with a flick of his wrist. "We're going on a treasure hunt, and the treasure is a birth certificate and adoption papers."

# CHAPTER 28

Bright sunshine warmed Heather's car until the automatic thermostat kicked on and cool air flowed from the air vents onto their faces. "The clouds must have cleared," said Steve. "That's one thing about December weather in the south. You don't know if you're going to need a coat or a short-sleeve shirt."

Miles passed without talking, nothing unusual when riding with Steve. Heather turned to the right as her car came to a stop. "Charles is punching in the gate code. Are you sure you know where to look for the adoption papers?"

"Pretty sure." Steve didn't sound as confident as she'd like. "I'll qualify my answer. I'm sure they're somewhere in the house. I'm ninety percent sure I know where."

He'd been pondering the missing adoption papers for over a week. Captain Loving had checked with the financial institutions. Blake didn't rent a safety deposit box in any of them, at least not under his name and Social Security number. The documents had to be in the house.

"This is quite a home," said Alexandria when they entered. "It reminds me of the broadcast studio."

Steve wiggled his nose like a bunny. "It needs a good airing out."

Captain Loving issued a challenge. "My men have gone through this place twice that you know of and once more for good measure. It's time for you to amaze us, Steve. Show us how a blind detective can find something a half-dozen sighted people couldn't find after three tries."

Heather added, "Don't forget, Bella and I looked. We did some serious looking before your deputies arrived the first time."

Steve tapped his way forward to the middle of the room and turned right. Sweeping right to left with his cane, he stopped when it hit a solid object. He reached with his free hand. "Here it is." He searched for the center of the display case of snakes and fumbled with a latch on the door. He opened it, traced around the hole with his fingers and inched his hand forward.

"This is so creepy," said Alexandria. "You're not going to put your hand in there, are you?"

"It only looks creepy to you," said Steve. His hand went in deeper.

"Keep going another six inches," said Heather.

His elbow scraped the glass as he inserted his arm until he felt the furry mouse. His fingers closed around the stuffed rodent. The sound of a spring releasing broke

178

the silence. Steve winced as something struck his hand with unexpected force. Alexandria screamed.

Nervous laughter followed as Steve held the stuffed mouse. He dropped it and felt the stand it had been placed on. Beneath it, his fingers touched tan Astroturf.

He pushed the turf aside and dug his finger in a hole. "There's something metal. It feels like a lever." He pushed it forward, but it didn't move. He pulled it. A loud click sounded. A trim piece hit him on his hips. He pulled out his hand and stepped away from the display.

"You did it," said Heather. "That released a hinged trim board below the glass. There's a thin metal box under the display."

"Take it to the table," said Captain Loving.

Steve followed the footsteps of the trio.

"Jackpot!" said Heather. "These are Bella's adoption papers."

"Anything else?" asked Steve.

"A birth certificate."

"Do they look legit?" asked Captain Loving.

Heather paused. "The adoption papers are styled correctly." She flipped to the last page. "The signatures are where they're supposed to be, and there's a stamped seal. We won't know for sure until we verify this through court records." Heather paused. "The birth certificate looks good, but I'm not sure what a birth certificate from Florida is supposed to look like."

"Florida?" asked Alexandria.

"Collier County, Florida," said Heather. "Wherever that is."

"It's in the southwest part of the state, near the tip of Florida, on the Gulf of Mexico side." Alexandria paused before she continued in a sheepish voice. "A long time ago, I dated a guy from Naples."

Captain Loving's voice came across as mock-accusation. "Any other old boyfriends you haven't told me about?"

"Don't start with me," cautioned Alexandria. "I just found out about you and Heather a few weeks ago."

Heather overcame the awkward moment with a question. "Who's going to put the mouse on his stand?" When Charles didn't volunteer, she did. Alexandria teasingly called her betrothed a coward.

Steve rested his hands on his cane. "If it's okay with you, Charles, I'd like for Bella not to know we found the adoption papers and birth certificate. We're looking for her birth parents, and we don't want to get her hopes up."

Charles considered the request for a few moments. "I'm not sure I can keep this quiet. These documents tell me Bella is a minor and Human Services needs to be contacted." He took a breath. "I might misplace them for a day or two."

"Thanks," said Steve.

"By the way," said Charles. "I found out on the way over here that Jolene Cox is returning a day early.

That's where my focus will be. Let's go to Blake's office and make copies for you."

## Chapter 29

T he next morning Heather's routine of doing research on her laptop came to a quick end when Steve called. Cryptic, guarded words told her he couldn't reveal what he wanted to say. The unspoken portion of the message meant she needed to take a quick shower and get next door as soon as possible. Steve needed rescuing.

Bella made an early appearance, threw a coat over her pajamas and headed to Steve's with Heather. "Is Gwen here already?"

"She arrived an hour ago," said Heather as she knocked on Steve's door.

Heather took in an extra-large breath when she viewed an artificial Christmas tree standing in the corner of Steve's living room. Brightly-wrapped presents dotted the floor around it. Garland hung from the fireplace mantle and a sprig of mistletoe dangled from the top of the door frame of the hall leading to the bedrooms. As much as the sights of Christmas being celebrated in Steve's world had taken her by surprise, what astonished her more was the Christmas music pouring from his television.

"Are you ready?" asked Heather.

Steve rose from his recliner and moved to the front door. "Let's go." He stopped, turned, and said in a cheery voice, "You two behave."

Gwen rose from her pile of wrapping paper and presents. "You didn't tell me you were leaving." She approached Steve and gave him a kiss on the cheek. "Should I be jealous? You're leaving with a beautiful woman. Are you keeping secrets from me?"

"Of course, I'm keeping secrets. It's Christmas."

Bella giggled.

Steve slipped on his coat and wrapped his neck with a scarf. Once outside, his demeanor chilled like the early morning air. On the way to the car, he said, "Go to the office. We need to work on the case."

Heather had heard him use the same tone before. It didn't necessarily mean bad news, but it did mean he'd found out something important. "Who called you?"

"Captain Loving. Someone tipped off Child Protective Services. They know Bella is only sixteen. He's turning over copies of the birth certificate and adoption papers to them."

Heather clicked her key fob to unlock her SUV. "There will be an emergency hearing today, and they'll place Bella in temporary foster care. Shouldn't we stay with her?"

"No. Go to the office. I can't think with that stupid Christmas music blaring in my ears."

Twenty minutes of silent travel later, they arrived at their office. Steve spent another thirty minutes drumming his fingers on his desk while nursing a cup of coffee. With no preamble or warning, he stood and began to pace. He stopped after three trips across the office and back. "Heather, have you made any progress with your research?"

Heather kept looking at her computer monitor. "Not much. I contacted the National Center for Missing and Exploited Children. A search of their database didn't result in a hit. They recommended I get a DNA sample from Bella and send it off for analysis. I did that a few days ago."

"How long until you expect results?"

"I requested paternity, maternity, and full ancestry. The lab I chose said five to seven business days for Bella's mother and father. It will take six to eight weeks for a full workup. Should I call and see if they can expedite the process?"

Steve shook his head, which meant he'd already moved on in his mind. "We know the county in Florida where the birth and adoption were supposed to have taken place. Let's call a private eye in Collier County and have him check it out."

Steve began to pace again. "This case is driving me bonkers. What's the motive for killing Blake Brumley? Is it hatred, plain and simple? Did Blake cheat Jolene Cox out of a fair divorce settlement? If so, Detective Schmidt may be right. Jolene may be the killer." He ran his fingers through his hair. "I still have questions about Olin Field. He said he bought an expensive airplane and was left holding the bag. How expensive was it? Is he trying to sell it?"

Steve paced. "I'm not convinced Olin told the cops the truth about where he was during the murder. We need to talk to him again."

"There's another possibility," said Heather. "We know Dart Salinsky was grooming a dog at the time of the shooting. Could he have had one of his animal rights buddies on the roof with the rifle?"

Steve stopped in his tracks. "That's a possibility, but I'm not convinced Dart Salinsky is that cunning. I'd put the probability at less than ten percent. The caliber of the rifle is wrong. Only a big game hunter would own one. The drop of the projectile was over thirteen inches. I just can't see an animal rights activist knowing enough to adjust elevation."

Steve spoke into his cell phone, "Call Olin Field."

After five rings, Olin sounded harried when he answered, "Field Electrical Supply, this is Olin."

Steve laced his words with heightened concern, "Olin, Steve Smiley here. Heather and I wanted you to know we found Bella's birth certificate and adoption papers late yesterday afternoon."

"Where were they?"

"In the snake display. There's a hidden compartment."

Olin's response seethed out of him. "That sneaky son of a gun." He gathered himself and asked, "What happens to Bella?"

"That's the bad news. The cops were obligated to call Child Protective Services and tell them Bella is a minor. Heather believes she'll be placed in foster care today."

Olin's voice rose. "Why can't she stay where she is?"

Heather answered. "I'd have to be a state-approved foster parent to be considered. That involves training I haven't received and jumping over a mountain of procedures."

"I see."

Steve asked, "Will you be at your business this afternoon? We'd like to come by and visit with you."

His words came out clipped. "Come whenever you want. I have to go. Customers are standing five deep."

Steve settled at his desk. His cell phone announced a call from Gwen. As he usually did when he and Heather were together, he put it on speaker so she could hear and participate in the conversation.

As soon as he tried to speak, Gwen cut him off with cracked, high pitched words. "Steve, you have to help her. They came and hauled Bella away. They threatened to arrest me if I interfered. What can we do? I need to be with her."

"Take a deep breath, Gwen. The one thing you don't need to do is get yourself arrested. We know you love her and only want the best for her. She's in no danger."

They heard Gwen take a deep breath and let it out into the mouthpiece. "I'm sorry. It happened so fast. They treated me like I had kidnapped her."

"Heather and I found out about CPS being told only a little while ago." Steve paused. "I knew the police had to notify CPS, but I hoped it wouldn't be until tomorrow."

Heather interrupted. "There's a chance the adoption papers and birth certificate are phony. Who would know for sure?"

"Jolene Cox."

"Yeah," Steve whispered in a tone that indicated he agreed with her. "From what you've told us she didn't have much to do with Bella, but she should know. Blake realized what an asset he had in her and perhaps Jolene did too. I can see where Jolene would want Blake out of the way so she could cash in on Bella." Steve paused. "What about Olin Field?"

"Olin? I don't know." Her voice warbled with hesitation. "I doubt it, but now that you mention him, he might be involved."

"Yes?" said Steve as a way of asking her to continue.

"He was with Blake and Jolene when they adopted Bella. At least that's the story I heard. He's a good man,

187

but paranoid when it comes to laws and rules. That goes double since he was arrested. He would know better than anyone Bella is under-age. He might have been trying to get ahead of the police by calling CPS."

Steve took over the narrative. "I see what you mean. He might have tipped off CPS to avoid being asked why he didn't tell the cops how old Bella is. He had to have known."

Gwen circled around to a question she'd already asked. "What can we do to get Bella? She'll go nuts if she doesn't have Mike."

Heather made sure to soften her voice. Her next words would sting enough without her sounding void of compassion. "Unfortunately, there's not much that can be done in the immediate future. Child Protective Services has exclusive jurisdiction. I studied the divorce decree. Jolene did not relinquish all her parental rights. She did give Blake custody and signed papers giving the proceeds from Bella's earnings to Blake. She might make a claim for Bella now that Blake is dead. That opens up another basket of problems. The police are on the verge of arresting her for murder. I can't see CPS approving her living with Jolene until there's no question of her involvement in Blake's death. Then there's the issue of her not being a part of Bella's life. CPS will be acting *in loco parentis*, in the place of the parents. It's a shame you aren't an approved foster parent."

The phone went silent, but not for long. Gwen spoke with determination, "What does it take for me to be a foster parent?"

Steve leaned forward and rested his elbows on the desk. "Are you sure you want to make that big of a commitment?"

"I've been doing it for years. We could live in Bella's home like we did before, except Blake wouldn't be there."

Heather said, "Go online. I've not studied the latest requirements. They tend to change frequently."

"I'll do it now."

The line went dead.

Steve stood with his white cane in hand. A partial smile tugged on the corner of his mouth. "I'm in the mood for a spicy Chick-Fil-A sandwich and some waffle fries."

His words came out buoyant, even expectant. Heather tented her hands on her hips. "Is eating all you can think about? A minute ago you were pacing the floor and acting despondent about the progress we're making. Now you're ready to dive into lunch. How can you change gears so fast?"

"It was a matter of time before the truth about her age came out. I'm glad it did. It gave the pot a thorough stirring. Something useful is bound to come to the surface." He strode to the door. "Get your questions ready for Olin Field. He'll be our first stop after lunch."

# Chapter 30

After circling the Chick-Fil-A parking lot twice, Heather found an opening and swung her car into the vacant spot. The hum of voices filled the restaurant as she led Steve to a booth. "Don't rest your elbows on the table until someone cleans it."

A smiling grandmotherly woman with a name tag that read "Beula" followed them with a rag and spray bottle in hand.

After placing orders, Heather returned to the table with drinks and a blue rectangular box about the height of a liter of water. "Feel this, Steve. These are color-coded, so the wait-staff know which table to deliver the food to."

Steve ran his hands over the box. "How do they keep the orders straight?"

"Beats me, but they do." She took the cover off his straw and stuck it in his drink. "Diet Coke is directly in front of you."

Steve took a drink and leaned forward. "Did I tell you I hired a P.I. last night?"

Heather dipped her head, looking out of the top quadrant of her eyes. "I think I'd remember that small bit of information."

"I meant to tell you first thing this morning, but my place turned into a little bit of a zoo. Gwen came over and started decorating the living room. Mike was wrestling with wrapping paper, Gwen was telling Max to leave the ornaments alone, and to top it off, she fired up the Christmas music. I couldn't think for the noise."

"Enough with the apology. Tell me about the P.I."

"The guy is in Naples, Florida, and is verifying the birth certificate and adoption papers. He said he'd get on it today."

"What if they're not legitimate?"

An eager-faced server delivered their meals. Heather removed the plastic cover from her salad.

"Umm," said Steve after he tasted the fried potato. "To answer your question, I'll be surprised if they are legit."

Heather stopped her fork half-way to her mouth. "Why do you say that?"

"Blake was only two years into his television show when Bella joined the family. The financial records you read to me indicated he wasn't into big money during the early years."

"What's your theory?"

Steve took a huge bite of his sandwich. A sliver of lettuce fell to the table. Heather moved it out of the way without saying anything. She took two bites of her salad while Steve ate another waffle fry and wiped his mouth.

"I think Blake hired someone in Florida to fake a birth certificate and adoption papers from Collier County. I also think he staked out another place in Florida where he would be sure to see little girls with blonde hair and the girls' parents."

Heather caught his train of thought and wondered why she hadn't thought of it. Steve had already taken another bite, so she filled in the gaps. "Blake had to get a look at the mother and father to see what the girl might look like once she was grown. He did child selection and abduction by profiling."

Steve nodded but kept chewing. Heather said, "We should be looking for tall, blonde parents with striking blue eyes." She stopped to ponder. "Why Florida? Bella could have come from anywhere."

Having swallowed his most recent bite, Steve said, "It's possible anywhere came to him."

"Huh?"

Steve rested his forearms outside the boundaries of his meal. "Once it's verified the documents we found yesterday are forgeries, we need to focus on Orange and Dade counties in Florida. We need to look for abducted girls aged eighteen months to four years."

"Why those counties?"

Steve's shoulders rose and fell. "Call it an educated guess. If Maggie and I had a little girl that age, I'd want to take her to Disney World, Universal Studios, or on a family cruise. Orange County for the first two and Miami for the cruise." He reached for another fry. "We may have to expand our search, but those counties should be a good place to start."

Heather rested her fork on a napkin and stared at Steve. He'd managed to put himself with his wife in the role of loving husband and father, even though they had no children. She wondered again why they made that decision. Previous attempts to draw information out of him had resulted in a terse, "We didn't want to." Heather collected her thoughts and said, "I'll call the Center for Missing and Exploited Children as soon as we hear from your P.I."

A passing mother carrying a baby in a sling across her chest caught her eye. Two children with missing teeth followed in the woman's wake. A fourth child lagged behind, sucking on a straw, oblivious to the world around her. How easy it could be for parents to lose track of a child, especially if someone intentionally distracted them.

Steve pushed the container of fries toward her. "Try one; they're great."

"No, thanks. I have more salad than I can eat."

Steve shrugged. "When we get back to the office, we need to do some detective work. Let's find out if Blake, Jolene or Olin made trips to Florida in the years that fit the time frame. We're looking for destinations of Orlando, Miami, and Naples. Also, we need to see if Olin or Blake owned or leased a private plane during those years. If so, it's possible Blake and Jolene used it to bring Bella to Texas."

Even though Heather had arrived hungry, the discussion of abducted children and having a plan on how to proceed curbed her appetite. She clipped the plastic top shut on the remnants of her salad. "From the photos of airplanes in Olin's office, I can almost guarantee he owned an airplane." She took a drink of her iced tea. "Whenever you're ready, I'm finished."

Steve continued with his meal. "I told you to get something besides rabbit food. Who wants to eat salad when you can have a spicy sandwich and fries?"

# CHAPTER 31

An aging Chevy cargo van sat alone in the parking lot of Field's Electrical Supply. "Looks like the rush is over," said Heather. "There's only one vehicle here. We should have Olin to ourselves."

Steve nodded and unlatched his seat belt. The twang of vintage country music filtered into the parking lot as the front door swung open. A tall man with gray whiskers, dressed in coveralls held the front door open for them. Olin looked anxious to see them and waved the duo back to his office.

"Don't you need to work the counter?" asked Heather.

"Things slow to a crawl this time of the afternoon. Emma will be back from lunch any minute. That was her husband you walked past on your way in."

"I take it he's an electrician," said Steve.

"He is, but he's not getting around like he used to. A fall off a ladder last year messed up his leg. It's hard to be an electrician if you struggle to climb a ladder. I work him here as often as I can afford to. Clyde and Emma can run this place better than I can. He's been after me to sell him the business ever since he got out of rehab. "

"Will you sell?" asked Steve.

"I'm mighty tempted, but where would I go? I'm not sure I can make enough money flying charters."

Heather glanced around the office. It hadn't changed since their last visit. Olin and Steve continued to chew the proverbial fat. Heather directed Steve to a chair in front of a desk topped with electrical catalogs that looked like medium-size phone books.

"What's the latest on Bella?" asked Olin.

"She hasn't sent you a text?" asked Steve.

"Yeah, she sent me a couple. She's not happy. Says the woman that came with the deputy is a real witch." Olin paused. "That doesn't sound like Bella. I think she's upset about Mike. She loves that dog and doesn't sleep worth a hoot without him."

"He's special," said Steve. "Mike and Max get in my lap at the same time. After a rocky start, I think they believe they're brothers."

Steve let a moment pass before he eased into the questions he needed to ask. "Olin, we need some help in trying to find Bella's birth parents. When did you first meet Bella?"

He lifted his chin and looked at the ceiling. "I first saw Bella at Blake and Jolene's home in Conroe about fourteen years ago. Blake had bought the land at Cut and Shoot but hadn't started on the lodge yet."

"You didn't fly them to Florida to pick her up?"

Heather paid particular attention to Olin, looking to see if she could detect any deception or hesitation in his answer. He responded without missing a beat and didn't look away. "Blake flew himself. He was a good pilot. I owned the plane but Blake pretty much paid for it. We flew the wings off that Cessna Skylane. We went all over the country and even into Canada and Mexico. I did the filming of the hunts."

Heather's chair made a loud squeak when she leaned to the right. "Are you sure Jolene didn't go with Blake to get Bella?"

A smile crossed Olin's face. "Jolene flies commercial unless there's no other way to get to remote locations. She hates single-engine aircraft. I'm positive she didn't go on that trip with Blake."

"Did you see her while he was gone?" asked Steve.

Olin again cast his gaze at the ceiling, as if he tried to look into the past. "Blake was gone for ten days, and her flying with him wasn't an option. Someone had to stay and answer the phones."

Steve moved right into the next question. "What plane did you buy before Blake told you he didn't want you around anymore?"

Olin gave out a grunt. "That's a kind way of putting it. He accused me of stealing some of his gold."

"Did you?" asked Heather.

Steve softened her question. "Forgive Heather. She experiences culture shock from time to time. Between her

197

training as an attorney and her time as a Boston cop, she learned to be rather direct." Steve smiled wide. "She asks the same questions I do, but she does it with fewer words."

Olin relaxed his shoulders and looked directly at Heather. "I'll give you a Boston answer to your question. No."

Steve said, "You said Blake flew by himself to get Bella in a Cessna Skylane. What's your new plane?"

Olin shifted his gaze to Steve. "We decided to get a Beechcraft Baron. It's a twin-engine aircraft with seating for six. That includes the pilot and whoever is in the right seat. It has a range of almost fifteen hundred nautical miles. Blake had graduated to a professional cameraman and considered hiring a sound technician. He needed something bigger and with a longer range."

"It sounds nice," said Steve.

"It's a honey, but not near as nice as what we looked at."

"What was that?"

"A Beechcraft King Air. It has seating for ten and a range of seventeen hundred twenty nautical miles."

"Why didn't you get it?"

"Even a four-year-old model costs over three and a half million."

"Ouch. I had no idea that's what planes sold for. How much was the Baron?"

"About one and a half million."

Steve leaned forward. "I checked out your alibi for the time of the murder. You have nothing to worry about. Six witnesses said you were at Conroe North Regional Airport preparing your airplane for takeoff. I also checked out your flight plan. You flew to Fredericksburg. Why did you go there?"

"The Hangar Hotel," said Olin.

"The what?" asked Heather.

"The Hangar Hotel is a fly-in hotel with a World War II vibe. It has an old-style diner next to the hotel where you can get a bite to eat. Park your plane, walk thirty yards, and step into a time warp. They even host dances every so often in a building that looks like a hanger. It's in Fredericksburg, a sort of touristy town not far from President LBJ's ranch on the Guadalupe River. It was founded by German immigrants, and you can still get authentic German food there. It's also the hub of Texas' wine industry. The main street is lined with places where you can taste what's produced from local vineyards." He paused. "It's been on my bucket list for a long time."

Steve nodded. "My wife and I spent a weekend in Fredericksburg once. We had a ball and didn't get to see everything we wanted to. We said we'd go back."

Heather quickly changed the subject. Memories of Maggie tended to knock Steve off his game.

"Olin, do you think Bella's adoption was kosher?" asked Heather.

The muscles in his jaw tightened. "Are you asking if I think Bella was kidnapped?"

Heather nodded. "Either that or something involving a lot of money and a shady adoption."

He took his time responding. His gaze fixed on a photo on the wall. "Something wasn't right. Neither Blake nor Jolene ever mentioned they were adopting. Out of the blue, Blake returned with a pretty blond girl and said they'd adopted her. Jolene took care of Bella for a while, but being a momma wasn't for her. After the lodge at Cut and Shoot was finished, Blake hired Gwen. Jolene moved out but continued to go on some of the hunts and take care of the logistics. She worked from her apartment in town. She got enough money from the divorce to start her own business. That ended her relationship with Bella."

"Did you go on the international trips?" asked Heather.

He nodded his head and swept his hand again at his surroundings. "My business suffered, but I went where Blake and Bella went."

"What's your impression of Gwen?" asked Steve.

Even though Steve had asked the question, Olin looked Heather straight in the eye. "Gwen loves Bella every bit as much as I do." He glanced over at Steve. "And that's a lot."

# CHAPTER 32

The trip back to the office didn't require or invite conversation. Steve sank into the leather seat of Heather's car and played the part of a statue. His silence meant he'd heard something that required concentration enough to fit a piece, or pieces, into place. His phone rang. Instead of putting it on speaker, he held it close to his ear. After traveling a mile on blacktop through a forest, he gave a short, "Thanks," and disconnected the call.

Instead of slipping the phone into his coat pocket, Steve gave an instruction to the device. "Call Charles Loving."

"Captain Loving," This time Steve had his phone on speaker.

"Charles, this is Steve Smiley. We hired a P.I. in Collier County, Florida. He's been to their courthouse. Bella Brumley's birth certificate and adoption papers are phony. We don't have a clue who she is or how old she is."

A groan sufficed for a response. Charles asked, "Are you anywhere near Conroe?"

Heather spoke. "We just left Olin Field's business."

"Stop by. Detective Schmidt is on his way with Jolene Cox. Give me the details from your investigator, and I'll let you listen in on the interview."

The trip didn't take long. A fax machine ground out the last copy of the report submitted by the Florida investigator. Captain Loving gathered the pile, tapped them on his desk until the edges lined up, and slipped a paper clip over the top left-hand corner. He looked at Heather. "You need to give this guy a bonus. The sheriff's office detective I contacted told me it might be several days until he could look into it."

"We're not opposed to paying top dollar for good work," said Heather.

Captain Loving looked toward the door. Detective Schmidt leaned against the door frame. "I put Jolene Cox and her mouthpiece in the interview room," he said with disgust.

Steve said, "I take it she didn't have much to say on the trip from the airport."

Schmidt let out a sarcastic huff. "She talked. She said, 'On the advice of my attorney, I'll answer no questions until he's present.'"

The trio trailed Detective Schmidt down a bright hallway. Captain Loving opened the viewing room for Heather and Steve. They stood shoulder to shoulder in front of the glass.

"Tell me what she looks like," said Steve.

Heather stared at Jolene Cox and sounded like a radio dispatcher. "Female, early forties, dark hair, five-foot-four-inches tall."

"More description on the hair," said Steve.

"Coal-black, no gray, cut short, think Beatle Paul McCartney in mid-sixties, complete with sweeping bangs."

"Got it. Keep going."

"Her skin looks burned by wind and cold. Plenty of wrinkles. Her hands are in her lap under the table. No glasses. Keen eyes of indistinguishable color. She's sitting erect but relaxed. No signs of stress."

"What's she wearing?"

"She's wearing a light-green long-sleeve shirt under a tan hunting vest. Dark green cargo pants fit loosely over hiking boots. Little or no makeup."

The preamble to the interview ended, and Captain Loving led things off. "I want to emphasize, Ms. Cox, that you are not under arrest. You may terminate this interview at any time."

While Captain Loving took care of conveying redundant information, Jolene's attorney, Jack Blackstock, glanced at the top page of a document in a file he'd brought with him. He closed the manila folder. "Fire away. Ms. Cox is here to cooperate. However, Captain, I'll give you fair warning that I won't tolerate any shenanigans like the warrant you secured to search her home. If you'd waited, she would have given you permission."

Heather looked at the attorney. He sat in the chair like he didn't have a care in the world. Dark wavy hair covered the tops of his ears. A close-cropped beard rested under brown eyes with flecks of gold. She gave him a second, longer look. He wore a white dress shirt with the top button unbuttoned. A silk tie hung loose, at the ready to be tightened into a knot if a formal occasion required it.

"Ms. Cox," began Detective Schmidt, "can you explain how a rifle belonging to you was found on top of a pet store on the Saturday after Thanksgiving?"

She looked at her attorney. He nodded for her to speak. "No, I can't. I left that gun at the home of Blake Brumley over ten years ago."

"Can you prove that?" asked Schmidt.

Jack Blackstock may have looked loose and comfortable, but he replied with steel in his voice. "Do you have evidence to the contrary? If not, she's answered your question, and you need to move on."

"He's good," said Steve.

Heather nodded, even though Steve couldn't see her.

Schmidt wasn't through with questions about the rifle. "Why did you leave your rifle behind when you moved?"

Again she looked at her attorney, and again he nodded.

"The rifle wasn't mine. The manufacturer gave it to Blake so he could show it being used on his show. I happened to be handy when they needed a signature." She locked her gaze on Detective Schmidt. "Have you ever shot a .416 magnum?"

He gave a curt, "No."

"Blake picked it out, and it fit him, not me. I know rifles, Detective. I wouldn't have used that one."

"Why not?"

"I told you, it fit Blake, not me. It's designed for short-range shots at huge, dangerous animals. You have to fit your cheek on the stock and take aim without searching for the front sight."

"Next question," said Jack Blackstock. His tone indicated he believed the queries about the rifle had been squeezed dry.

Captain Loving spoke before Detective Schmidt pursued the dead-end any longer. "Ms. Cox. What did you think when you received word Blake was suing you, claiming you violated a non-compete clause in your divorce agreement?"

Steve raised his head. "I didn't know that, did you?"

"I missed that one," said Heather. She focused on the attorney, who allowed his client to speak.

Jolene placed her palms flat on the table. "After watching Blake pull dirty deals over the years, it didn't surprise me one bit. It also didn't surprise me when the judge threw the case out."

"Speaking of divorce," said Detective Schmidt. "Are you aware we found nearly two million dollars in gold hidden in Blake's home?"

If loathing could be expressed by the sound of a person's voice, Jolene Cox had it mastered. "I'm not surprised you found it, but I would have guessed cash, not gold. Blake denied he owed me money through the divorce. I suspected he made deals to launder income from manufacturers through foreign accounts, but I couldn't find the proof. I didn't give him credit for taking an extra step and converting the cash into gold."

Detective Schmidt glared at Jolene. "How much of that money do you think you were cheated out of in the divorce settlement? A million? That sounds like a good motive for murder to me."

Jack Blackstock reacted like a coiled spring being released. "I think we've had enough of backdoor accusations wrapped around speculative motives. Let's cut to the chase and talk about opportunity. At the time of the murder, Ms. Cox was at ROOTS, a Beauty Salon in Spring." He opened the file, turned it around, and pushed it toward Captain Loving. "I'm providing you with time-stamped security photos and depositions from three cosmetologists and four customers. Each person will swear my client was at that location at the time of the murder."

Jolene pointed to her head. "The main thing I took from my marriage to Blake Brumley was gray hair. I don't like gray hair." She looked Detective Schmidt in the eye. "I didn't like Blake, but I didn't kill him."

"Scratch one suspect," said Steve. "Let's see if we can buy an hour with Ms. Cox and Jack Blackstock, Esquire."

# CHAPTER 33

A converted single-story home sufficed for Jack Blackstock's law office. It sat alongside a busy four-lane city street, flanked by an insurance company on one side and a chiropractor's office on the other. By way of explanation to Steve, Heather said, "It looks like one of those streets that started out as a two-lane and had to be expanded. The homes lost their large front yards and were rezoned mixed-use. What remains of Mr. Blackstock's front yard is a little grass and parking for three cars. There's additional parking in the back."

What was once the home's living room served as the law office's waiting area. A fifty-something-year-old woman sat behind a computer monitor and gave a warm smile. She wore glasses and possessed striking argent hair that brushed the collar of a burgundy blouse.

"Don't bother sitting," said the woman. "Jack called and told me to expect special guests. Follow the hall to the end." She stood and swept her hand toward the right side of the home. Much like her boss, she projected relaxed courtesy under deep waters of poise and dignity.

"I have a fresh pot of coffee brewing. How 'bout I bring you a cup?" asked the receptionist.

"That would be wonderful," said Steve. "Black for both of us."

The attorney's office door stood open. Jack Blackstock sprang from his seat as soon as Heather and Steve came into view. "Come on in," he said with a wave of his hand. The obligatory diplomas hung on one wall while a bookcase behind the barrister's desk held an impressive display of legal tomes. Four leather-covered chairs sat in an irregular circle in front of a polished hardwood desk. Jolene Cox occupied one of the chairs, looking relieved that the ordeal with the police had concluded without her being jailed.

On a far wall, a framed painting caught Heather's eye. She gave Mr. Blackstock an inquiring look that included raised eyebrows. He gave a thin-lipped smile and nodded an affirmative answer to her unasked question.

Heather touched Steve's arm. "Before we sit down, there's something I want to show you over here, Steve." Heather guided him across the room toward the painting. She took his hand from her shoulder and placed it on the edge of a picture frame.

"What's this?" asked Steve.

Heather cleared her throat. "It's a painting of ducks on the water at Herman Park in Houston. The artist signed it in the lower right-hand corner with the initials M.S. The M is surrounded by the swirl of the S."

Steve staggered and dropped his cane. He reached with his other hand and traced the frame. He managed to croak out, "Let me feel the signature." His fingers caressed the spot. After a silent thirty seconds, he said, "I remember when Maggie painted this. I was going through a tough time. I came close to quitting the force."

He turned from facing the wall. "Where did you get this, Mr. Blackstock?"

Through the door walked the receptionist carrying a tray with four cups. "He didn't. I did."

Jack took quick steps to the woman and relieved her of the tray. "Thanks, Mom."

Heather couldn't help but stare. The resemblance of mother and son struck her. Why hadn't she noticed it before?

With her hands freed, the woman approached Steve and Heather. "I didn't get a chance to introduce myself. I'm Cora Blackstock." She paused and placed a hand on Steve's forearm. "It's such a privilege to meet you, Mr. Smiley. You were at work the day I came to your home and purchased this from Maggie. She impressed me as a person who never met a stranger. We must have talked for two hours."

Steve reached out a hand, and Cora took it. Steve couldn't speak, so Cora tugged his hand gently and said, "Let's get you settled in a chair, Mr. Smiley."

"Steve," he croaked. "Please call me Steve."

Once Steve had settled, Jack handed him a cup. "Hot coffee in front of you, Steve."

The cup shook a little, but he managed not to spill any.

"You wouldn't happen to have any more of Maggie's paintings for sale, would you?" asked the attorney. "Mom's been kicking herself for only buying one."

Steve nodded. "As a matter of fact, I do. They're in a climate-controlled storage building in Houston."

Heather settled in a chair. "You never told me you had some of Maggie's paintings."

Steve shrugged. "I didn't know you were interested in them."

"How many do you have?"

"Ninety-six."

Cora gasped. "Do you have any idea what Maggie's paintings are selling for these days?"

Steve shook his head. "I didn't want to track it after she died. All I know is the insurance premiums keep increasing."

Jolene Cox took a cup of coffee from the tray and handed it to Heather. Cora gave Steve a final pat on the shoulder. "Please let Jack know if you ever want to sell any of Maggie's paintings. He's behind on his Mother's Day presents."

Cora excused herself and closed the door. Jack looked at each person and said, "As much as I don't want to, we'd better discuss what you came for. What's on your mind?"

Steve released a ragged breath before he began. "Heather and I are trying to find the biological parents of Bella Brumley. We're not here representing law enforcement in any way, but our investigation has uncovered something that may put Ms. Cox in legal jeopardy."

Jack's keen eyes narrowed. "And what might that be?"

Heather took over to give Steve more time to gather himself. "Bella's birth certificate and adoption papers are forged documents. They're convincing, but forgeries all the same."

Jolene shook her head. "That jerk. Why did I ever marry him?"

"Do the police know this yet?" asked Jack.

Heather nodded. "They also have copies of the report from the private investigator we hired."

Jolene asked, "Does this mean I'll be arrested?"

Jack's index finger bounced off his closed lips as he considered her question. He lowered his hand. "It depends on what they believe your level of involvement was in obtaining the child."

Heather noticed how quickly Jack, the easy-going art lover, changed into a keen-witted attorney.

Steve spoke while Jack seemed to be formulating his strategy. "We've developed a possible scenario of what Blake did to obtain Bella. It involves kidnapping. We don't think Jolene had anything to do with it or participated in carrying it out. Some of what we have to

212

say is speculation, but if we're right, Jolene will be well served to answer our questions. What we propose is for us to lay our cards on the table and have you advise Jolene if she should talk to us."

Jack nodded and looked at Jolene. "Are you comfortable in hearing what they have to say?"

"I survived a charging bull moose this week. Listening to a story doesn't seem very dangerous compared with that."

"You have our full attention," said Jack. "However, I'm advising Jolene not to respond to anything at this point."

"That's all we're asking," said Heather.

Steve reached out his cup for Heather to take. "This is going to take a while. We think the abduction took place in Florida."

Steve went on to tell of the origin of the adoption papers and their theory of abduction from an area where legions of parents with small children gathered from a multitude of states and countries. Steve shared the scant information Bella had offered as well as what they'd learned from Gwen Fontaine. Finally, the interviews with Olin Field were relayed as well as his being caught ransacking Blake Brumley's home and his subsequent arrest for burglary.

Heather joined in the conversation and spoke of the DNA testing and her contacts with the National Center for Missing and Exploited Children.

Jack grimaced. "Your theory is interesting. It might be true, but it's weak on facts. We need to find out who Bella is and who her birth parents are. Without them, it's going to be an uphill battle."

"What do you mean?" asked Jolene.

Jack shifted to look straight at Jolene. "It's called plausible deniability. The police aren't likely to believe you didn't know about the kidnapping or illegal adoption. At the very least they're going to think you suspected something was wrong, but you didn't report your suspicions."

Jolene looked to Jack as if she needed him to throw her a lifeline.

Steve said, "Our theory will sound like a fairy tale if we don't find Bella's parents. I'd like for Jolene to answer some questions we have that might help us."

"I'm not sure about that," said Jack.

"Why not?" asked Jolene.

"It would be best if you only told your attorney," said Heather. "Attorney-client privilege. If Steve or I were called to testify, we'd have to reveal everything we heard you say."

Jack issued something akin to a boy's mischievous grin. "There's another office next door if you two would like to make some notes. Don't feel bad if you leave a scrap or two of paper on the table. I'll make sure it's disposed of."

As everyone stood, Jack looked at Steve and Heather. "We three should get together for supper tonight and discuss this."

Steve said, "Count me out. I need some downtime with a lonely dog and a cat that gets snitty if he feels abandoned."

Jack raised an eyebrow and gazed only at Heather, "Looks like it's you and me, counselor."

She reached into her purse, pulled out a business card, and wrote her home address on the back. "Six-thirty, if that works for you."

He pocketed the card and allowed a smile to answer for him.

Once in the car and buckled in, she looked at Steve. "The last time you tried to play matchmaker, it didn't work out too well. Remember?"

"This may be a way for you to get rid of the Christmas present you bought for Charles. You told me on the way over Jack rated higher than Charles on your hunkometer."

"Hunkometer? Is that another of your made-up words?" She shook her head and started the engine. "I have to admit, he's not bad."

Steve drifted into another world. "Can you believe it? They have Maggie's painting."

# CHAPTER 34

Following a triplet of knocks, Steve opened the door to Heather's townhome. She slipped from her seat at the bar overlooking the kitchen, stood, and stretched. Heather exhaled a sigh of fatigue and frustration.

"Still nothing?" asked Steve.

Heather puffed out her cheeks and released a full breath of air. "For the last four days, I've been searching old newspapers, missing children reports and anything else I can find from Florida. I called people I know at the FBI, and they've called in favors from south and mid-Florida. It's been a complete bust. None of the theme parks or the cruise lines reported a child missing that fit Bella's description. I even expanded the timeline of the abduction. I'm beginning to wonder if we're barking up the wrong tree by looking in Florida."

Steve leaned his cane against the wall while Heather took steps toward the coffee pot. "Yesterday's interview with Jolene Cox didn't yield anything new that I noticed. Did you catch anything?"

"Nothing that could help us track Bella. Blake flew to Conroe fourteen years ago with a blond, tanned child barely out of diapers."

"Wait a minute," said Steve. "Bella came with a tan? I don't remember Jolene telling us that."

Heather poured Steve a cup. "Jolene's exact words were 'brown as a pinto bean.'"

Heather looked on as Steve mounted a barstool, faced her but didn't speak. She continued her report of their recent unfruitful inquiries. "Where was I? Oh yeah, our interview with Jolene. She said Blake flew in with a kid tagging behind him and she hit the ceiling. Can you imagine a husband that would come home with a child you had no prior knowledge of?"

Steve took his first sip of coffee and sat the cup on the counter. "I think she's telling the truth. She eventually moved out and left Blake to fend for himself with the child."

"Are you sure?" asked Heather.

"The more I listen to Jack's dictated notes, the more convinced I am she knew nothing of Bella coming. She's a unique, self-sufficient woman. I'm surprised she's not living in the wilds of Alaska in a log cabin with a pack of sled dogs. In fact, she talked about doing that very thing when you and Jack went to the next office and talked about legal strategy." Steve lifted his mug. "You were talking legal strategy, weren't you?"

Heather ignored the innuendo. She didn't want to feed Steve's imagination about her budding relationship with Jack.

Steve mused, "Why did she ever marry Blake?"

Heather quickly added. "Don't you remember? Jack asked Jolene the same thing. She told him she'd dreamed of hunting big game and Blake was looking for someone to handle the logistics and shoot birds for him. It was a marriage born of business, not love."

Steve raked a thumbnail across his chin. He'd sometimes do this as he digested a morsel of information.

Heather needed a break from concentrating on locating new information with the consistency of quicksilver. "I heard Christmas music coming from your side and voices earlier. Did Gwen come over again?"

Steve nodded. "She didn't stay long. It's part of her twice-a-day routine to see how our investigation is progressing. She's doing everything she can to fast-track her approval as a foster parent." Steve wagged his head. "Speed isn't something bureaucracies are known for."

"How is Bella?"

"Gwen says she hates where she's living even though the foster parents are nice enough. She'd be doing a lot better if she had Mike."

Heather stared at her computer screen, wishing the answer to Bella's predicament would arrive via e-mail. "I'm at a loss. What can I do next?" She raised her head after he didn't respond. His eyebrows had drawn together closer than she'd ever seen. "What is it?"

Steve left his coffee on the counter and zombie-walked to the living room. He eased himself into Heather's recliner and raised his feet. Minutes later, he came out of his self-imposed trance."

"Jolene said Bella arrived with a dark tan, right?"

"That's what she said."

"And you said we've been barking up the wrong tree by looking in Florida."

Heather walked to Steve and knelt beside him. "You have an intense look about you, Detective Smiley."

Steve lowered his legs. His words came faster than usual. "We have a lot to check, and I might be wrong." He rubbed his hands together. The atmosphere of the room charged with anticipation.

Heather stood. "Where do we start?"

"Find the flying range of a Cessna Skylane."

It didn't take Heather long before she found the manufacturer's specifications. "That year's model can fly nine hundred thirty nautical miles before refueling."

Steve nodded. "Go out nine hundred nautical miles from south Florida and make a list of places the plane could have landed. We'll need to check those islands for missing children that fit Bella's description."

Heather worked for an hour and said, "This is a big haystack. The Bahamas are well within range, the Dominican Republic is seven hundred and twenty nautical miles away, and San Juan, Puerto Rico is eight hundred and ninety-seven nautical miles from Miami. That airplane could have made it to any of them."

Steve and Heather spent the rest of the day searching for a child that went missing from one of the islands of the Eastern Caribbean twelve to sixteen years ago. They skipped lunch and only came together when Heather ordered a Grubhub delivery of supper and had it sent to Steve's townhome.

Mike and Max scampered through the pet door as soon as the delivery came. Heather left her computer where it lay on the bar and scurried next door through driving rain. She arranged the meal so Steve could attack it with no problems. He used a fork to stab General Tso's chicken from a white cardboard box and lifted a pork egg roll with his free hand. Heather used chopsticks to lift chunks of orange-glazed duck and fried rice. After a few bites, she made green tea and put the mug off to the right side of Steve's plate.

Steve broke his silence halfway through the meal. "I didn't hear you screaming for joy from any of your phone calls."

Heather stabbed a piece of duck but didn't raise it to her mouth. "I take it you didn't have much luck, either."

"I'm not giving up. The Eastern Caribbean is hours ahead of us, and a lot of government offices were closed when I called. We'll keep looking early tomorrow morning."

"And if that doesn't work?"

Steve shrugged. "We'll expand our search until we run out of ocean."

At one-thirty the following afternoon, Heather let out a scream. She beat a path to Steve's living room.

"Where?" asked Steve as soon as his door swung open.

Heather's hands shook. "St. Croix, U.S. Virgin Islands. It was a couple hundred miles past the range of the Cessna."

Steve said, "I should have known. He refueled somewhere." Steve paused. "Parents?"

"My buddy at the FBI said he'd call me as soon as he found out."

Steve took in a deep breath. The exhale of relief came with a word of caution. "There's so much we don't know yet."

Heather's phone rang. The voice coming from it gave her the information they'd hoped for. She expressed her thanks and signed off.

"Bella's mother and father are alive and well."

It became apparent Steve's mind had shifted into high gear. "Call him back. They need to get with the FAA and find the paper trail of Olin's plane into and out of St. Croix."

Heather took in a deep breath. "Take a breath, Steve. The FBI is all over this."

He nodded. "I'll call Captain Loving and Jack. We need to set up a meeting with them tomorrow morning at our office. We have a lot to do, and there's still a murder to solve."

221

Heather issued a word of caution. "If the parents sold Bella to Blake, it's going to crush her."

# CHAPTER 35

With only eight days left before Christmas, the McBlythe Professional Building glittered and blinked with holiday decorations. Instrumental carols and tunes of the season piped softly throughout the building and in the elevator. Heather wore a blazing-red sweater festooned with small brightly-wrapped boxes. A black skirt, complete with an appliqued Christmas tree, met the top of her black boots. A necklace of blinking multi-colored lights hung around her neck

She told Steve the new emerald-green sweater he wore was beige. She also failed to tell him about Santa's frowning face woven into it. Printed above Santa, it read: "No presents!" Underneath it read: "I've been naughty." Ugly Christmas Sweater Day at the professional building had come.

The festive mood of the office fit the season, but not necessarily what Steve and Heather had to discuss with their two guests. Jack Blackstock arrived first. He strode in wearing his usual business attire with the addition of a vest adorned with Disney characters in Christmas costumes. Captain Loving took one look at everyone, and said, "I didn't get the memo."

Heather put her index finger to her lips to shush him and mouthed silently as she pointed to Steve, "He doesn't know."

"What memo?" asked Steve.

"Nothing," said Heather. "Let's get started. Go ahead, Steve."

He groaned. "You put me in a silly sweater, didn't you?"

"Guilty," said Heather. "It's tame compared with what others are wearing."

Steve shook his head. "Christmas can't be over soon enough. At least we'll have one present that's worth giving. We located Bella's birth parents in the U.S. Virgin Islands."

Jack Blackwell's gaze snapped upward from his legal pad. "Are you sure it's them?"

Heather nodded. "I contacted a college buddy that's moving his way up the ranks of the FBI. The dates check out, and the agent received a photo of a two-year-old that shows the birthmark on her neck. The only thing remaining is to have experts verify DNA. Luckily, the parents preserved samples of hair after Bella went missing. We should know the results this afternoon."

Captain Loving pinched his eyebrows together. "I know a lady who's going to be upset if this checks out."

"Gwen Fontaine?" asked Steve.

"Yeah. Does she know Bella's parents have been located?"

Steve issued a quick, "No." He folded his hands together on the table. "Has she been hounding you too?"

"Twice a day she calls and asks for updates on our investigation. She knows the birth certificate and adoption papers are fakes, but we wanted to make absolutely sure before we told her. She's intent on being Bella's foster mom."

Steve rubbed his chin. "By the way, Charles. Did Captain Schmidt check out Gwen's alibi for the time of the murder?"

"She gave him a ticket stub from a tour of the LBJ ranch. It had a timestamp of 3:15 p.m. With holiday traffic, there's no way she could have driven that distance in less than five hours without getting a handful of speeding tickets."

Heather looked at Charles and shifted her gaze to Jack. "I heard from Judge Conner's office a little while ago. I filed a petition for an emergency hearing to release Bella from foster care. It's to take place at ten o'clock tomorrow morning."

Charles groaned. "I don't have to be there, do I? I have something important scheduled tomorrow afternoon."

Heather covered a chuckle. She knew that something important involved a short ceremony and rings that would be put away until after a spring wedding.

Steve leaned forward. "I called Alexandria while you were on your way. Since she's doing freelance reporting, I thought a nice Christmas story about a kidnapped daughter being reunited with her parents might be something she could sell. Judge Conner gave special permission to have the proceedings filmed." Steve paused a moment to let the words settle in. "Tomorrow promises to be quite a day."

# CHAPTER 36

Heather's heels clicked on the marble floors of an empty courtroom. She and Steve arrived a full forty minutes ahead of time. She settled him in a chair at a table usually reserved for the prosecution in a criminal trial or the plaintiffs in a civil proceeding. She unloaded a stack of papers from a black satchel and arranged them in front of her.

Heather looked at Steve and smiled. He wore a navy suit, white shirt and a red tie with images of the seven dwarfs in Santa hats scattered across it. What he didn't know wouldn't hurt him. She wore a shamrock-green business suit that accentuated her eyes, with a candy-cane striped scarf draped over one shoulder. Steve could be a fuddy-duddy about Christmas if he wanted to, but she would have none of it. Especially, not today.

She swiveled in her chair as the door at the rear of the courtroom creaked open. Jack Blackstock ambled in with his boyish smile. His greeting mixed the charm of a man without a care in the world with the formality of his surroundings. "Mornin', Steve." His smile broadened as he gave Heather a shoes-to-eyes once-over. "Counselor, you're looking particularly festive and lovely today."

"Thank you, sir. And may I say you look particularly dashing in your holiday vest and matching tie. I can honestly say I've never seen Dickens' characters from *A Christmas Carol* portrayed in such startling colors."

Steve lifted his chin. "Did you bring Jolene with you?"

"She's powdering her nose," said Jack, still looking at Heather.

Steve chuckled. "I doubt that. She may be loading powder into shells, but it's hard for me to imagine her using powder for anything other than a rifle or shotgun shell."

A noise at the door caused Heather to look over Jack's shoulder. Alexandria Ramos breezed into the room and scanned it. In her wake followed the same scraggly cameraman who had been with her at the mall when Blake's life ended. She pointed to a spot against a wall and spoke low enough not to be heard. The man nodded a mop of curly hair and schlepped his camera and tripod to the place indicated.

Heather smiled a greeting as Alexandria approached. After introducing her to Jack, she said, "You look exceptionally radiant today, Alexandria." Heather teased her with an arched eyebrow and said, "Something special planned?"

Full red lips parted into a conspiratorial smile. "Charles said he has something in mind this afternoon."

"Sounds interesting."

Alexandria looked over at the cameraman. "Work before pleasure." Her gaze shifted to Steve. "Thanks for the phone call, Mr. Smiley."

"Consider it an early Christmas present."

Charles Loving came through the door about the time Alexandria turned to join her cameraman. She beat a quick path to her soon-to-be husband. They met halfway and locked in a kiss. Not an easy task for a couple when the man stood a head and a half taller than the woman. The kiss lasted long enough for Jack to look away with raised eyebrows and mouth the word, "Wow."

When the clench ended, Charles made his way to the front of the courtroom. Heather reached into her purse and pulled out a tissue. Handing it to Charles, she said, "Your fiancé seems to have left a holiday greeting."

"Thanks. I may have to start carrying a handkerchief."

"Did Detective Schmidt come with you?" asked Steve.

"He'll be here in a little while. I thought it might be a good idea if he made sure Olin Field remembered to come."

Before anyone could respond, the door swung open again. Jolene Cox came forward and stood beside Jack. She wore her version of dress clothes: new blue jeans, hiking boots, a powder blue oxford shirt, and a down vest. Her short hair looked clean and combed, but slightly more like George Harrison than Paul McCartney. She didn't wear the slightest smear of makeup.

Jack pointed to a seat on the front row behind Heather. "Jolene and I will sit here. This shouldn't take long."

Heather took her seat and checked her watch. Only ten minutes remained before the proceedings were to begin. A portly bailiff and a court reporter entered by way of a door near the witness stand and took their respective positions. Heather turned to see Bella and a woman she assumed to be the foster-parent step into the courtroom. A stern-looking woman wearing a gray business suit and half-framed glasses herded the two as if she were an Australian shepherd. She directed them to the respondent's table, adjacent to where Steve and Heather sat.

As if a high tide had rolled in, people spilled through the door and flowed into the gallery where they took their seats. The courtroom filled to capacity. Subdued chatter sounded like a church congregation waiting for the call to worship.

Despite the firm instruction from Ms. Half-glasses, Bella left her seat and latched onto Heather with a two-armed hug. She whispered, "What's going on?"

Heather didn't have time to explain before the gray-suited woman stuck forth a hand and said, "Lucille Brown, Senior Case Manager. Bella needs to sit with me."

Bella ignored her again and worked her way around Heather. She leaned into Steve, whispering something Heather couldn't hear.

Lucille Brown glanced over and spoke in a voice that didn't invite objection. "Bella, you need to come to our table and have a seat." She pointed to the table reserved for defendants in a criminal proceeding.

Steve patted Bella's hand and said. "Mike's doing great. He misses you. Don't worry. You two will be together soon."

Olin Field, Gwen Fontaine, and Detective Schmidt filed in with only a minute to spare. Olin and Gwen sat behind Bella after they each exchanged hugs and received another scowl from the Senior Case Manager. Heather noticed Gwen whisper something to Bella that earned her only an 'I-don't-know' shrug of the shoulders.

At precisely ten o'clock, a door opened, and the Bailiff commanded, "All rise." The formal announcement of the judge's appearance and purpose came forth with the usual pomp. Robed in black, the man's silver hair lay on his head like a helmet. He huffed his way up a few steps and plopped into his chair. Donning a pair of glasses, he fumbled with papers in front of him.

After a dramatic pause, he glanced over the top of his glasses and asked, "Are the attorneys for the plaintiff and respondent ready to proceed?"

The door to the courtroom burst open. A man toting a briefcase took long steps toward the judge. He wore a wrinkled suit. His over-the-ears hair looked as if he'd not had time to run a comb through it, let alone wash it. "My deepest apologies for being late, Your Honor."

He tried to begin another sentence, but the judge cut him off with a slash of his hand. Judge Conner pointed to a spot on the floor in front of him. "Stand right here, son, and quit groveling."

The man did so. Heather gave a short prayer of thanks that it wasn't her standing before the judge.

"Do you own a watch, son?"

"Uhh, no, sir. I use my phone."

"I see." He leaned forward. "I want you to write a letter to Santa. Ask him for a watch. That phone doesn't seem to keep time."

"Yes sir."

"Are you the attorney for Child Protective Services?"

"Yes sir."

"Did you read the petition provided by Ms. McBlythe?"

He swallowed. "Not yet Your Honor. Due to the haste with which this hearing was scheduled, I haven't had...."

Judge Conner barked out, "Quiet!" He stared icicles at the attorney. "Young man, I've heard excuses for the past thirty-two years. Some of them were pretty good. I even give mercy points for originality. It only took me a half-sentence to know you have nothing to add to my memoirs." He leaned forward across the judge's bench and sniffed.

"Son, have you been drinking?"

The portion of the attorney's ears Heather could see turned pink. "No sir."

The judge squinted and sniffed again. "What time did you leave last night's Christmas party?"

Heather leaned into Steve. "He's busted."

Steve nodded and made sure his voice couldn't be heard. "I smelled it when he passed by."

The judge settled in his chair and stared at the disheveled attorney. "To keep you from a perjury charge, I'll withdraw my last question. I'm in too good of a mood to let you ruin my day." He looked out on the gallery and raised his voice. "At high noon, I'm hanging up my robe and going to a retirement luncheon. The only reason I agreed to Ms. McBlythe's petition for an emergency hearing is that I thought this case would be a good way for me to end my career." His gaze sharpened even more on the young attorney. "I'll not have this day spoiled because you didn't think this case was worthy of proper preparation or because you stayed out to the wee hours doing God knows what."

Heather stood. "Your Honor, may I approach the bench?"

He looked at her. "Come on."

Both attorneys stepped forward as far as they could. The judge covered his microphone with a vein-streaked hand. Heather spoke loud enough for him to hear, but not without him cupping an ear with his free hand. "Your Honor, it's obvious my colleague needs to be brought up to speed on this case. I propose you allow me to put my business partner on the stand and have him relate the pertinent details of the case before the court."

The judge nodded and turned to the rebuffed legal representative. "Any objections?"

"Not as long as I can ask questions."

"I'll allow it. Stand back."

Heather called Steve to testify and the bailiff swore him in. Before Heather could begin, the judge turned to Steve. "Mr. Smiley, can you tell a story without bloviating?"

"I'll trim the fat and give you nothing but lean, Your Honor."

The left corner of the judge's mouth pulled up. "My kind of witness. Proceed, Ms. McBlythe."

Heather thanked Judge Conner by name and said, "Mr. Smiley, relate the pertinent facts concerning the matter before the court, namely, the custody of a minor child known as Bella Brumley."

Steve took a deep breath and began. "On Saturday after Thanksgiving, around noon, Ms. McBlythe and I were walking to the entrance of The Woodlands Mall. A shot rang out, and Ms. McBlythe grabbed Bella Brumley and guided her and me to safety. The shot killed Blake Brumley, Bella Brumley's father by adoption. In the course of the afternoon, Bella asked if Ms. McBlythe would act as her attorney and also retained Ms. McBlythe and me to find her birth parents." He paused. "I should add that we are both registered private investigators."

Heather looked over at the other attorney. He had the brief she'd submitted to the court and was running his finger down the page, something he should have already done.

Steve continued, "The home of Blake Brumley was searched multiple times by officers from the Montgomery County Sheriff's Department. Ms. McBlythe and Bella Brumley assisted them on two occasions. Despite their best efforts, nothing relating to Bella's true identity was found. We did one final search and found a birth certificate and adoption papers. These documents proved to be falsified. That's when we realized we were most likely looking at a case of child abduction."

The attorney sitting next to Bella asked, "Has law enforcement verified this?"

Heather didn't hesitate. "The falsified documents have been verified by a private investigator, a detective from the Collier County, Florida Sheriff's department and the FBI." She added, "You'll find your copy of the forged documents in the attachments, as well as the reports from the private investigator we hired and the law enforcement agencies I mentioned."

If Heather hadn't been looking at the attorney, she wouldn't have noticed the door at the rear of the courtroom open. A smartly dressed man in a dark suit led the way. He directed a tall, slim, tanned man and a woman who looked like an older clone of Bella to sit on the back row. Heather turned and nodded at Alexandria. The camera turned to take in the couple whose gazes had locked on the young woman with long hair so blonde it appeared white.

The judge prompted Steve to continue.

"That left us at square one in our investigation. The only clue we had was a county in Florida. We concentrated on the major theme parks and cruise lines in that state. We tried to place ourselves in the shoes of the kidnapper and looked at places rich with children as targets. In a subsequent interview with a witness, we learned that when Bella arrived in Texas, she had a deep tan. We also knew that Blake Brumley had full access to an aircraft with a range of nearly a thousand miles. Florida became our first place of interest."

The judge interrupted. "Am I to conclude Blake Brumley kidnapped the young woman seated here and pretended he was her adopted father?"

Steve gave his head a nod. "Yes, Your Honor. He even went as far as to have a forged birth certificate and adoption papers produced. With those, he obtained a Social Security card and a United States passport in the name of Bella Brumley."

Steve took in a deep breath and continued. "Florida seemed to be the most likely location of the abduction, but we were wrong. Our search there proved fruitless until we realized it would be easy enough to refuel in Florida and go on to one of the many islands in the Caribbean."

Steve paused. The room grew eerily quiet as people leaned forward. Even Judge Conner sat spellbound.

"Two days ago, Ms. McBlythe found what we'd been looking for. Fourteen years ago, a two-year-old girl went missing from a resort owned by her parents in St. Croix, The U.S. Virgin Islands. In a newspaper account, a father described his daughter as an adventurous little girl who loved the ocean. After an extensive search, it was assumed by authorities that she wandered from the resort into the water and became a victim of the ocean."

Heather glanced at Bella. Tears, not the fake ones she'd been taught to shed, tracked down her face.

Steve kept going. "We can only surmise the details of the abduction, but FAA records show the plane flown by Blake Brumley traveled from Texas to Florida. From there it flew to the Dominican Republic, refueled, and arrived in St. Croix three days before a blond-haired, two-year-old girl went missing. Blake Brumley flew out of St. Croix the same day he abducted the toddler and retraced his path to Texas."

Heather turned to the respondent's table. "For the benefit of my colleague, I'd like to state that those documents are found in a separate addendum."

The judge looked over his glasses. "Continue, Mr. Smiley."

Heather used the occasion to look into the gallery. Her gaze made it no further than to Gwen Fontaine. Her rosy complexion had turned sallow. Unblinking eyes fixed on Steve.

Steve's next words pierced the room. "The young woman we know as Bella Brumley did not drown. She was abducted by Blake Brumley and flown to Conroe, where she became his adopted daughter. He groomed her to be a TV personality, specializing in killing big game animals. As she matured into a beautiful television star, he saw an opportunity to exploit her even more. A bullet stopped him from carrying out his plans."

Judge Conner turned to face Steve. "Mr. Smiley, do you know the true identity of Bella Brumley?"

"Yes sir. Her name is Holly Swenson, and her true date of birth is December the eighteenth."

"Her birthday is today?"

"Yes sir. She's seventeen years old today."

The courtroom erupted in gasps and muted conversations.

# CHAPTER 37

Judge Conner rapped his gavel to bring order.

Heather looked to the young woman they knew as Bella and now knew was Holly Swenson. She sat with mouth agape and eyes wide and crying. Heather shifted her gaze to the judge. "Your Honor, a special agent with the FBI is in the courtroom. It's my understanding he has with him the results of DNA testing that proves beyond doubt Lonnie and Ingrid Swenson are the true and legal parents of Holly Swenson, also known as Bella Brumley. With your permission, I'd like to add these to the documents I've already provided the court."

"Granted." The judge looked into the gathering. The man with the close-cropped hair, clean-shaven face and nice suit stood. "FBI Special Agent Daniel Russell. Permission to approach Sir?"

"Granted."

"Permission to bring Lonnie and Ingrid Swenson with me?"

Holly shot to her feet. Decorum went out the window as Ingrid Swenson ran down the aisle, to be met halfway by her daughter in a collision of hair, tears, and moans of, "Momma. Momma. Momma!"

The arrival of Lonnie Swenson added more tears as a father's sunbaked hands reached around both wife and daughter, drawing the family into a complete unit after fourteen years.

Off to the side, a sound arose like something from a haunted crypt. It started as a low, "No." The one-word sentence repeated itself over and over, growing each time in intensity and volume. "No. No. No. No. No!"

Eyes focused on Gwen Fontaine. After bellowing the same word three more times, her eyes flashed. She pushed away from Olin Field's restraining hand. "I'm her mother!" she screamed. "I raised her. She's my daughter."

Olin reached for her again.

"Get your hands off me." Her eyes went wild with fury. Detective Schmidt and two deputies moved in. The FBI agent held out his hands to block Gwen from the reunited family.

Steve stood, found his way from the witness stand and bumped into the desk where Heather stood watching. "Get me closer to Gwen," he said.

She led him to a spot a couple of yards from the sobbing Gwen. Instead of soft words, Steve spoke in a firm voice. "You can't have her, Gwen. She's not yours. She never was."

Something dark and malevolent shot from Gwen's gaze. "What do you know? You didn't even know I was leading you on. You were so easy."

Steve's voice held the kindness of a jail key. "Don't kid yourself. I suspected you from the first day."

"Ha! That's a laugh."

Steve's reply came in short bursts. "It was you that taught her how to shoot. You were the only one that could give her daily lessons. Olin had his business to run. And he was off with Blake a lot of the time. You learned about adjusting for wind and elevation from professional marksmen. You taught it to Bella."

"You're wrong again!" she screamed. "I taught myself those calculations, and I taught Bella."

Steve pressed on. "You knew about the .416 Remington Jolene signed for. You knew she would be suspected. You knew she was an expert shot with a rifle."

He paused long enough to take a breath. "I have to admit, calculating that a 400-grain bullet would drop nineteen inches at two-hundred-fifty yards was quite an accomplishment."

Spittle shot out as she shouted, "That round didn't drop nineteen inches; only twelve and a half. I put the front sight on the top of the skull and..." She froze in place.

A shroud of silence covered the room. Judge Conner's gavel fell like the blade of a guillotine. "Take that woman into custody."

Steve stepped back with his hand out until Heather guided him from the fray. Gwen only managed to mumble repetitions of the word 'no' as a deputy snugged handcuffs over two shaking wrists. Too stunned or too worn out by her tirade, she didn't resist.

Jack made room for the Swenson family to sit together behind Steve and Heather. Three raps of the judge's gavel brought the courtroom to order after Detective Schmidt herded Gwen Fontaine out a side door. The judge looked at Steve and Heather and gave a toothy smile. His gaze shifted to the attorney sitting next to the sour-faced case manager.

Judge Conner's smile disappeared. "Before I make a ruling in this matter, do either of the attorneys have anything to say?"

The disheveled attorney exchanged whispers with the case manager.

Heather announced, in a clear, firm voice, "No, Your Honor."

The attorney charged with protecting the interests of the State rose to his feet. "Your Honor, I'd like to remind the court that before a modification of placement out of foster care can take place, there needs to be a full investigation."

The judge slammed down his gavel. "Counsels, approach the bench." He glared at the man in the rumpled suit. "Mr. Grimes. Bring that woman you've been whispering to with you."

Heather looked into eyes that blazed like coals from a campfire. Again, Judge Conner covered his microphone with his hand. His words came out slow and low. "Mr. Grimes, I'm going to ask you a series of rhetorical questions. Don't answer them."

The young attorney silently nodded his head.

"Do you realize there's a camera filming these proceedings? Do you also realize that in thirty-five years on the bench I've never allowed the proceedings of my court to be filmed prior to today?"

He lifted a stack of papers from his desk. "I realize you didn't think it worth your time to read and study the evidence provided to this court pertaining to the abduction of the minor previously known as Bella Brumley, but I did. The evidence is compelling and overwhelming. The DNA evidence put the icing on the birthday cake for that young woman and her parents."

Out of the corner of her eye, Heather saw the lawyer's Adam's apple bob.

The judge leaned forward a little more. "In the gallery, I'm looking at a camera that's capturing what we say and do. If I were a betting man, I'd say these proceedings will be shown on national news tonight. I'm also looking at a lady I recognize. She's an author who writes extensively about missing and exploited children. I'm also looking at another lady I know. She's the director of the Dallas branch of the National Center for Missing and Exploited Children. And finally, I'm looking at the parents of Holly Swenson. I have a question for both of you. Why are you trying to make me look like the Grinch who stole Christmas with some hogwash about needing to conduct a silly investigation?"

The case manager straightened her shoulders. "We have rules and procedures that must be followed."

The judge took his gavel with his right hand and caressed the head of the mallet with the long, thin fingers of his left hand. He covered the microphone again. "Ma'am, you don't seem to understand where this is heading. This is my last case. I've already decided what I'm going to do. The only thing that remains to be seen is if you and Mr. Grimes are going to be held in contempt of court and spend Christmas in jail."

"You can't do that," snapped the woman.

The judge raised his gavel, but before he could slam it on the desk, Mr. Grimes squealed, "We have no objections or comments, Your Honor. We apologize for interrupting the proceedings."

Judge Conner took his hand off the microphone. "Let the record show that the State has no objection to the court making its final determination. This court finds that Lonnie and Ingrid Swenson are the true and lawful parents of Holly Swenson, previously known as Bella Brumley." The gavel fell.

Judge Conner descended and motioned Heather to come to him.

"Yes Sir?"

"Get the family over here. I want you to take a picture of me with them." He winked. "Thank you for allowing me to end my career on a good note."

With no cases to follow, the courtroom became a photo gallery and professional interview site for Alexandria. She interviewed those desiring to be interviewed and a few that didn't.

Heather sidled up to Steve. "Good job, partner."

Steve nodded, but it didn't convey complete satisfaction. "Did Dart Salinsky make an appearance?"

Heather looked toward Alexandria as she shook hands with the author who wrote extensively of missing children. Dart stood off to the side, waiting to get his next shot at publicity. "He looks like he's waiting to be interviewed."

"Is Detective Schmidt in the courtroom?"

"Yes. He must have had a patrol officer take Gwen to jail."

"Ask Detective Schmidt to come here."

Heather caught Schmidt's attention and beckoned him with a smile and a crook of her finger.

Steve dipped his head, listening for heavy footsteps. "Detective Schmidt, can I ask you a question or two?"

"Sure."

"Did you ever find out who made the phone call that tipped off Alexandria to come to the pet store and be near the entrance of the mall?"

He issued a sigh. "Not yet. We're sure it's a man's voice on the recording Alexandria gave us, but it went through a filter."

Steve issued a noncommittal, "Hmmm." He shifted his weight to his other foot. "What about the store's surveillance video?"

"The whole system went down the morning of the shooting. The manager came in at ten o'clock that morning. It wasn't operating until Monday when a repairman found a wire in the office had been cut."

"That's what I thought," said Steve. "Heather checked out the camera monitoring the rear of the store. That one scanned the back door and the ladder to the roof. She didn't think it had been tampered with."

"I know," said the Detective. "We also checked that camera."

Steve had another question. "Did you ask who closed the store the night before or who opened the store on that Saturday morning?"

"No. I assumed it was one of the assistant managers."

Steve's eyebrows lifted. "You might want to find out. Were you aware Dart Salinsky is such a trusted employee he has keys to the store?"

Detective Schmidt jerked his head in the direction of Dart and squinted. "No, I was not aware he had keys to the store."

Steve leaned forward. "Detective, do whatever you want to with that bit of information, but if it were me, I'd do more investigating before I arrested Dart."

"Why's that?"

Heather said, "He's slippery. He thinks playing tag with the police is a game."

Schmidt nodded. "Any other reason?"

Heather glanced at Dart and brought her gaze back to Detective Schmidt. "If I were Gwen Fontaine's attorney, I'd be looking for someone to share the blame. Painting Dart as the brains behind the killing would be a defense that could mitigate her sentence. Who knows, he may be the mastermind behind the plan. He had plenty of motive."

Steve added, "The DA will be much more interested in getting two convictions than one. Gwen's testimony against Dart in exchange for a reduced sentence should do the trick."

The detective's gaze fixed on Steve. "Does Captain Loving know about this?"

Steve reached out a hand for the detective to shake. "This is our Christmas present to you. Charles knows nothing about it."

"Thanks. I mean it. Thanks a lot. I couldn't ask for a nicer gift." He looked at Dart and smiled. "Any more surprises out of you two?"

# CHAPTER 38

After Alexandria finished the interview with the author, she came to Heather and Steve. "You're next."

"Do I have to?" asked Heather.

"We both do," said Steve. "This will be part of her dowry. She'll sell the footage to the highest bidder this afternoon."

Alexandria nodded with emphasis, her eyes shining, full and bright with excitement. "He's right. This story has everything: a nationally known TV star, child abduction, private detectives solving a murder, a dramatic courtroom scene, and a family reunited at Christmas. It will go national and international." She moved closer and whispered. "The author I interviewed is all over this. She's talking to Lonnie, Ingrid, and Holly about a memoir. She told me she's looking at partnering with a screenwriter and selling the movie rights. If that happens, they'll need my video, which will be another revenue stream."

Steve adjusted his sunglasses. "Wow. A movie? Heather and Holly could play themselves, but who wants to see me? They'd have to get someone that wouldn't make children cry."

Both Heather and Alexandria scolded him for his self-deprecating quip.

Charles Loving walked up and wrapped his arm around his betrothed. "Honey, I need to get to my office. How long will this take?"

She looked around the courtroom at who else needed to be interviewed. "At least another two or three hours. We'll need to edit the footage and show clips to the media outlets. Then the bidding starts. That won't take long after the networks and tabloids find out what I have. I may have to go to our appointment dressed like I am, but I'll be there on time."

He gave her a squeeze. "Don't expect me to look any different, either. I don't want any mistakes made with Gwen."

Steve cleared his throat to indicate he wanted in on the conversation. "Charles, I'd like to ask a favor of you. Could you give Heather and me about fifteen minutes alone with Gwen before you talk to her?"

Heather looked on as Captain Loving ran a hand across his face. He paused a long three seconds.

Heather gave him a reason to agree. "I'll assure her the interview won't be recorded. Steve will be assisting me."

Charles threw his hands skyward. "Why not? She wouldn't be in jail if it weren't for you two. I'll see you at my office."

Steve asked, "Is Olin Field still here?"

"Sure is," said Charles. "He's waiting to talk to the Swenson family."

"Would you ask him to stop by your office?" asked Steve.

Heather noticed Charles' expression change from relief to suspicion. "Do you think he had something to do with the abduction?"

Steve shrugged. "I'll only say there are loose ends."

"I'll make sure he comes." Charles gave his bride a pre-nuptial kiss and made for the door.

Jack Blackstock sidled next to Heather. "Are you and Steve free for lunch?"

"Afraid not. We're on our way to the sheriff's department to try to put some bows on this Christmas present. How about supper?" she asked with raised eyebrows.

"Without me," added Steve with emphasis.

A smile sufficed for Jack's response.

"I do have a favor to ask of you," said Heather. "Would you mind running the Swenson's to my townhome? I'll be sleeping in Steve's extra bedroom until we can arrange transportation for them to return to St. Croix."

Heather followed Jack's gaze to the mother and father. Holly had an arm wrapped around each of their waists.

"They look tired," said Jack.

"Losing someone you love will do that to you," said Steve.

Holly and her parents came toward them and embraced both Steve and Heather in extended hugs. "You two are awesome," said Holly. She released Heather and put a little distance between them. "This may sound crazy, Miss Heather, but I don't want to see Gwen spend the rest of her life in prison." Her eyes added an extra measure of pleading to her next words. "She's been so good to me. Would you please represent her?"

Heather reached out her hands, and Holly grasped them. "I'm sorry, but it's not possible. I've been neck-deep in this case. No judge in the country would let me represent Gwen. At the very least I'll have to give a deposition. If it goes to trial, I'll have to testify." She paused and glanced at Jack. "I happen to know an excellent criminal defense attorney that might be willing to take the case."

Jack looked into the faces of each of the family members. All three nodded. He straightened his tie. "If you'll excuse me, I need to inform my client she's not to say anything to anyone."

Heather placed a hand on his forearm. "Steve and I were going to talk to her."

Jack shook his head. "Sorry, counselor. No dice. You're not to question my client."

Heather shifted her gaze to Holly. "That's exactly what you're looking for in a good defense attorney."

Steve took a step toward Holly. "We need to catch up with Captain Loving right now. Call Uber or Lyft to take you to our townhomes. You'll stay with your parents at Heather's place tonight. Heather will sleep in my spare bedroom."

# CHAPTER 39

A deputy sheriff motioned with his head as he said, "Mr. Field, Captain Loving is ready for you in his office." As usual, Heather walked with Steve's left hand on her right shoulder as his cane searched for objects in front of him. Olin asked, "Do you know what this is about?"

"I'll tell you after we get settled," said Steve.

Charles had arranged chairs in front of his desk by the time they arrived.

After settling into place, Steve faced Olin. "I'm hoping you can explain a few things concerning Blake Brumley's murder."

Olin nodded as he ran his hands down his blue jeans. "I thought that's what you wanted." His voice came out low and shaky.

"When did Gwen start coming on to you?" asked Steve.

Heather and Captain Loving traded glances. Steve's question seemed more like a statement that was common knowledge. Even though she knew it to be a common interview technique, it took Heather aback all the same.

"How did you know?" asked Olin.

"Gwen wears a brand of perfume I'm familiar with. You wear cologne that's subtle but distinct. She gave me a peck on the cheek once. I smelled both."

Olin shifted nervously in his chair. "Gwen called me not long after Blake fired her." A blush rose to the scar on his face. "She's always been like a smoldering fire to me."

"And for her?"

"Nothing in the past. After I was no longer welcome by Blake, Gwen and I kept in touch. It started with infrequent dinners. They became more frequent."

"What did you talk about?"

Olin shrugged. "General things."

"Like Bella, or, should I say Holly?"

"Yeah. We talked about Holly."

"That's not all, was it?" said Steve. "Gwen didn't like Blake backing out of the deal he made with you. He left you holding the bag for a new twin-engine airplane that cost one point five million dollars."

Olin slumped in his chair. "It started in July after he fired me."

"When did Gwen first mention the gold?" asked Steve.

"September."

Steve folded his hands together. "He fired her after he fired you. Is that correct?"

JINGLE BELLS, RIFLE SHELLS

Olin looked at Steve like he should have been wearing the robe of a prophet. "You figured it out, didn't you?" He kept talking when Steve didn't respond. "She first mentioned trying to find the gold after I let it slip about how I knew he was hiding it. I'd known about it for years. It had to be somewhere in the house. She found it, and she gave me enough to keep making payments on the airplane until I could sell it."

Captain Loving shook his head. "And maybe she took a little for herself too."

Olin turned his head like a puppy. "She's not a liar. She took enough for me to make payments for several months. She might have killed Blake, but she wouldn't steal for her own gain."

"I find that hard to believe," said Captain Loving.

Olin sat straight, ready to defend her. "Gwen knew Blake shafted me on the airplane and I had payments due beginning in August. She found the stash of gold in a return air vent in Blake's office. She took enough of it for me to make payments for six months. She didn't keep any for herself. Blake must have counted it and found some had gone missing. He blamed her, fired her, and found a new hiding place."

Captain Loving pointed an index finger at him. "So, you two decided to keep looking. That's when you broke in and began searching. That's why you sliced open the chair."

"She had nothing to do with that. I did it on my own. She chewed me up one side and down the other when she heard what I'd done."

Steve's head bobbed. The room remained still until he said, "Why were you intent on hanging on to the airplane?"

"It was for Bella. I was trying to get into Blake's good graces again. I hoped things could return to how they were."

Heather noted that he'd slipped into calling Holly by the name Blake had given her.

Olin kept talking. "Gwen wanted Bella's career to keep going, but not in the direction Blake planned. I have to admit, I wanted the same thing."

Charles shook his head. "Your story has a big hole in it. The plane would have to sit for a year, and there are strict travel restrictions on foster children."

Steve shook his head in disagreement. "Gwen was willing to wait. Remember, she knew the producers and directors of the shows. She was plotting out a new career for Holly that didn't include skimpy bikinis."

Heather added, "Gwen also counted on us not finding the birth certificate or the adoption papers. Even after things started to unravel, she must have assumed Blake paid for an illegal adoption from parents who valued money more than a daughter. It's hard to imagine a public figure who would kidnap a little girl in order to put her on television years later. Even a scoundrel like Blake Brumley."

Steve jumped in. "Holly's in line for a heck of a lot of money. That kind of money can buy influence. I bet Child Protective Services could make travel exemptions for a seventeen-year-old foster child who happens to be a television star."

Heather directed her gaze to Olin. "Did you suspect she wasn't as old as Blake made her out to be?"

"I didn't know for sure how old she was. I can tell you what a four-year-old deer looks like, but not a two-year-old child."

Steve rested his elbows on his thighs. "One more thing, Olin. Tell me about the trip you and Gwen took to Fredericksburg."

Olin swallowed hard. "You figured that out, too."

Captain Loving and Heather looked at each other, then fixed their gaze on Olin.

"It was Gwen's idea that we fly to Fredericksburg. I told you about the sweet little airport hotel that caters to pilots."

"Back up a little," said Steve. "Let's get the timeline of events in order. Blake Brumley was shot at noon. You were already at Conroe North Regional Airport. When did Gwen arrive?"

"You already know I arrived at about ten in the morning. Gwen said she needed to take care of something, so she drove her own car. It couldn't have been later than twelve-thirty when she stepped onto the tarmac. I had the plane ready to go, and we were in the air in no time."

Olin glanced at Heather and Charles and answered an unasked question. "I know what you're thinking. Why didn't I put it together sooner?"

Charles nodded.

"I drive a nineteen-year-old pickup that starts to complain if I go over sixty. It takes me at least forty minutes to get from the mall in The Woodlands to the airport, and that's in light traffic. She must have been driving eighty or more to get there so quick. I thought there was no way she would have time to get to the airport if she shot Blake."

Captain Loving added, "Most of the police force was responding to the shooting at the mall, which was the opposite direction to the airport. So if she was speeding, most likely there was no one there to catch her."

"When did you arrive in Fredericksburg?" asked Steve.

"Gwen wanted me to push the plane to see how it flew flat out. From wheels up to tires on the runway, it took about an hour."

"How long would it have taken you to drive it?"

"Beats me. I'd rather take a beating than drive that far on a holiday weekend."

Steve said, "After you landed in Fredericksburg, you rented a car and drove to the LBJ ranch, didn't you?"

He nodded. "Gwen said she wanted to see it. It's only a fifteen-minute drive from the airport in Fredericksburg. We weren't in a hurry, so we checked into our rooms first."

Heather gave Olin a piercing look. "Why didn't you tell Steve that Gwen went with you to Fredericksburg?"

Olin looked at a spot on the floor, then, raised his chin. "You may not believe this, but Gwen has strict boundaries when it comes to relationships. She didn't speak of it, but I think her ex-husband abused her something awful. As much as I wanted more, there wasn't anything but friendship between us." He looked around and must have seen skepticism. "It's true. Check the hotel. She had her room, and I had mine. I knew how it would look with us flying off and staying in a hotel." He dropped his head again. "I didn't want to say anything that would make people think less of her."

"You wanted more?" asked Heather.

Olin shrugged. "Look at me. I'm not what women call a good catch." An expression that begged for understanding came across his scarred face. "I guess you could say Gwen adopted me as a big brother. After the trip to Fredericksburg, I came to realize that's all I would ever be to her."

Steve said, "Gwen adopted you like she did Bella. She formed her own family when hers fell apart."

Silence.

Olin looked at Captain Loving. "Do I need to call my lawyer?"

Steve spoke before Captain Loving could. "Give him a break, Charles. He's telling the truth. Gwen is a lady until she perceives a threat. Even as handsome as I am, she pulled away when I touched her hand."

Heather and Charles looked at each other and had to cover their mouths to stifle a laugh.

Charles quickly said, "She tried to use you, Steve."

"Are you sure about that? I think she tried to protect the girl she believed to be her daughter. When Holly went into foster care, Gwen quit spending time at my townhome. The only thing she ever checked on was Holly. The tree, the presents, the music—it was all for Holly."

"What about the stolen gold Gwen gave him?" His finger pointed at Olin.

Heather used her attorney's voice. "There's no record of ownership. That might have been a gift from either Gwen or Holly. If I were defending Olin on that charge, I'd insist you prove it wasn't Blake's or Holly's gold to give to Gwen as they pleased. In fact, you'd need to prove it didn't belong to Gwen in the first place."

Charles shifted in his chair. "That's thin considering what Olin has told us."

Heather countered with, "He can't say for certain who owned the gold, and you can't prove who did."

Charles didn't appear to be convinced, but he moved on. "I can prove Olin flew a murderer to the other side of Austin after she killed Blake Brumley."

Heather went into full defense attorney mode. "Olin's recording of the timeline of Gwen's arrival at the airport is perfectly plausible. Any reasonable person would have reached the conclusion she didn't have time to do the shooting and get to the airport in thirty minutes. The rest is speculation on your part."

The room went quiet except for faint chords of music coming from a distant office. Charles fixed his gaze on Olin and stood. "No lawyer today. If what you've told us checks out, you should be in the clear." He rose and extended a hand to Olin. The grip caused Olin to grimace. Charles looked him in the eye. "If you don't testify against Gwen, I'm coming after you."

Olin promised to tell the truth when called upon to do so, thanked the trio, and left the room.

Steve stood after the door closed and stuck out his hand to Captain Loving. "Send us an invitation to the wedding next spring."

Heather winked and said, "Enjoy your evening."

# CHAPTER 40

Heather awoke to muffled voices. She pushed her sock-covered toes toward the foot of the bed in Steve's spare bedroom. A white sheet and duvet inched away from her face as she thrust both arms toward the ceiling. Her thoughts went to the previous night's dinner with Jack and the toe-curling kiss that ended their date.

Steve and Holly's voices moved from the hall into Steve's bedroom. The jingle of a dog collar followed. Heather's eyebrows pinched together as she threw back the covers and slipped her winter robe over flannel pajamas. She opened the door, wiped bits of grit from the corners of her eyes, and stepped in the direction of Steve's room.

"Are these the only shorts you have? They're ancient," said Holly.

"What you see is what I own."

Heather looked into the room. "What's going on? Why are you packing Steve's suitcase?"

Holly spun and greeted her with a smile and hug. "Steve's going home with me. Isn't it awesome?"

Heather shook her head to make sure she'd heard correctly.

Steve withdrew some socks from his dresser. "Drink a cup of coffee or two, and I'll give you the story."

He spoke to Holly. "Go check on your parents. I heard them coming alive next door. Tell them we'll have breakfast over here."

Holly, dressed in skinny-jeans, one of Heather's Princeton sweatshirts and a camo vest, shot out of the bedroom. The front door slammed.

Steve had already showered, shaved, and dressed. He wore navy cargo pants and a short-sleeve, loose-fitting shirt with a tropical print. White socks and tennis shoes completed the ensemble.

Heather led the way as Steve followed her to the kitchen. She poured a mug of Costa Rican dark roast and set it to cool. "What's going on?"

"We're cooking breakfast for our guests, and you're taking us to the airport. They own a hotel in St. Croix and invited me to spend the holidays. We fly to Miami this afternoon, spend the night, and tomorrow, it's on to the Virgin Islands."

Heather tented her hands on her hips. "Why is this news to me?"

Steve pulled his head out of the refrigerator. "You primped until Jack came for you and didn't get home until early this morning. The way you were humming, I didn't think you wanted to hear about my travel plans." He paused. "There's supposed to be yogurt and fresh fruit in here. Could you find it and put it out?"

With a voice laced with sarcasm, she asked, "Anything else?"

Steve chuckled. "As a matter of fact, you may want to get the pad and pen off the counter and make a list." He waited a few seconds and asked, "Ready?"

"Fire away."

"You'll need to get the burglary charges against Olin dropped."

"Are you serious?"

Steve buried his head again in the refrigerator. "Don't worry, it won't be hard. I called Judge Conner last night. He agreed to be your co-counsel. When I explained Holly is the sole beneficiary of Blake's will, he asked if she'd be willing to give an affidavit to the effect that she'd given Olin permission to come on the property any time he wanted and had permission to take anything he wanted."

Steve took a step back and huffed. "Holly put the groceries away last night. I can't find a thing."

Heather and Steve traded places. From over her shoulder, she heard, "You'll need to knock out something for Holly and her parents to sign. Fax it to Judge Conner. He'll talk to the D.A. You don't need to do anything else but make sure Olin is free to travel."

"Wait a minute," said Heather. "You're talking a million miles an hour, and I haven't touched my coffee."

"No time. You need to help me pack. First, let's get breakfast ready."

Heather pulled a bowl from the cabinet and began to crack eggs. "Why did you decide to go to St. Croix? How long will you be gone?"

Steve settled on a barstool. His voice dipped to a tone that meant he had something important to say. "I don't hate Christmas. I hate sitting alone at Christmas. All I can think about is Maggie. You have no idea what she was like this time of year. She was what made Christmas for me. This trip will allow me to be around different kinds of people, the sun, and the sound of the ocean."

Heather felt a stab in the area of her heart. Sometimes she wanted to fold her arms around Steve and whisper soothing things to him. She swallowed her words and scraped a tear from her cheek.

Steve spoke at an accelerated pace. "Besides, you and Jack will want to be together. You've already made plans for Christmas Eve and Christmas Day."

Heather slammed an egg against the bowl's edge, sending shards of shell into the mix. "How do you know we made plans?"

"I called and woke him this morning. He told me you were opening presents with his parents on Christmas morning. It doesn't take a genius to figure out you want to be with him the night before." Steve paused. "That

265

reminds me, I want you and Jack to go to the storage building in Houston where Maggie's paintings are stored. Look for the one that's the sister to the piece that's hanging in Jack's office. Maggie meant for them to be sold as a pair." He chuckled. "I didn't really think you'd want to give Jack a gift you intended for Charles. That's almost like re-gifting."

Heather stopped digging shell pieces out of the yellow goo. Her voice dropped. "Are you sure?"

Steve didn't hesitate. "Positive. Get one for you, too. Anything that catches your eye. Have Jack wrap it and stick a big red bow on it."

Heather gasped. "I don't know what to say."

"Don't say anything. Keep fixing breakfast. We don't have much time."

She dragged two frying pans out of a lower cabinet and put a flame under them. Soon, the smell of sausage frying filled the air. "Put some bread in the toaster," she said once her chin quit quivering.

"One more thing," said Steve. "You and Jack are coming to get me."

Heather stopped stirring the eggs. "Coming to get you? When you return from St. Croix?"

"No. Holly doesn't want Mike flying commercial. The day after Christmas you, Jack, and Mike will climb in that twin-engine Beechcraft Baron. Olin will point it east to Florida, refuel and it's on to St. Croix. We'll celebrate the New Year with Holly at her parents' resort, and Olin will fly us home."

Excitement rose in Heather like water coming to a boil. Steve had devised a plan worthy of a four-star general. The drumming of his fingers on the countertop indicated he wasn't finished.

"This can wait until we get back, but you're going to help Olin sell his business to Miss Emma and her husband. Olin doesn't know it yet, but he's moving to St. Croix to be Holly's pilot. She's planning on doing the fishing show and will need him for frequent island hopping."

"You weren't kidding when you said I needed to make a list."

"One last thing," said Steve. "Would you get rid of that tree and the decorations? I plan on traveling every Christmas for the foreseeable future."

Heather tilted her head. "That's not a bad idea. Where are we going next year?"

Steve issued a wicked smile. "Someplace with a nice murder to solve."

Dear Reader,

Thank you for reading a Smiley and McBlythe Mystery. I know your time is precious and I'm very grateful you chose to spend some of it reading one of my books.

There are a couple of things you can do to keep good, clean mysteries coming your way:

- Take a few minutes to write a review. Post it at your favorite online retailer and websites where readers gather.
- Recommend this book to a friend in person, at a book club or on social media.

You, the reader, are the reason I write. I'd love to hear from you. You can drop me a line from the contact page on my website at brucehammack.com.

Happy Reading!

Bruce

# About the Author

Drawing from his extensive background in criminal justice, Bruce Hammack writes contemporary, clean-read detective mysteries. When not writing, he enjoys reading a classic mystery, watching film noir movies and travel. Having lived in eighteen cities around the world during his life, Bruce Hammack now lives in the Texas hill country with his wife of thirty-plus years.

To find out about his latest release, sign up for his Preferred Reader email at: brucehammack.com.

Find him on social media:
Facebook.com/BruceHammackAuthor/
Instagram.com/brucehammackwrites

# The Smiley and McBlythe Mystery Series

## EXERCISE IS MURDER
### Book 1

How can a blind man solve a murder?

Steve Smiley's friend, attorney Ned Logan, is found at the bottom of his exercise pool. The police believe it was an accident. Smiley believes it was murder. But to prove it, he needs eyes…and a driver.

Heather McBlythe is trying to escape the long arm of her rich, influential father when she meets Smiley. His unorthodox proposition will buy her the time she needs.

Together Smiley and McBlythe set out to find a killer. Suspects abound. Can they find the killer before he strikes again? Will Steve be the next victim?

# THE LONG FALL
## Book 2

Twelve stories is a long fall.

Four classmates arrived in town for their twentieth high school class reunion. Now one of them is dead. Did he decide to end it all from the twelfth story? Or was it something more sinister?

Private investigator Steve Smiley and his partner, Heather McBlythe, are called to a posh Houston hotel to give their opinion. Steve no longer has his sight, but he still sees red at the scene of a homicide. And this one is definitely red.

Everyone close to the victim has a motive for killing him...AND an alibi. In the midst of unraveling the mystery, Steve and Heather are blindsided by opposition from a surprising source. Can they unmask the killer and bring justice, or will this long fall prove to be the perfect murder?

# THE ICE HOUSE MURDER
## Book 3

A Russian National sits in jail.
Someone with deep pockets wants him out.

Proclaiming his client's innocence, a Houston lawyer wants Smiley and McBlythe to find out who really committed the murder in the ice house. Steve's suspicions are aroused because the wily lawyer isn't known for representing innocent clients.

Smiley and McBlythe agree to take the case, and the exorbitant fee being offered, on one condition: that truth will prevail. Even if that means the Russian cooling his heels in jail is guilty.

Smiley and McBlythe have ten days to pinpoint the killer before the lawyer does things his way. The clock is ticking.

Then the unscrupulous lawyer ups the ante even more with a kidnapping. Time is short and the list of suspects long. Can Steve and Heather untangle the line of lies and deceit before another murder happens?

Made in the USA
Monee, IL
01 November 2019